JACK
THE
BAD CROW

JACK THE BAD CROW

HOLLY JO FLORA

Jack the Bad Crow

Copyright © 2023 by Holly Jo Flora

ISBN 979-8-9882508-2-1

All rights reserved.

Illustrations by Kim Sponaugle

Cover typography and design by Julie May

10   9   8   7   6   5

To My Sister, Manda

CONTENTS

CHAPTER 1

Johnny, Alex . . . and Jack

"Jack isn't bad! He's just . . . misunderstood. He's been through a lot," said Johnny as he hopped over to a large tree. Johnny was helping his best friend, Alex, gather pecans.

"Yeah, I know. And I feel bad for him, but I don't want to hang out with that crow just because we feel sorry for him. I mean, he acts like he's *so* much better than us," Alex grumbled as he added more pecans to their pile.

"My mom told me that today is Jack's birthday and he's lonely," Johnny said as he sat down by the tree.

"Lonely? How does your mom know he's lonely?"

"Jack's mom told my mom. His mom is worried about him. She said he lost all his crow friends when she and Jack moved into the barn. And I don't think he sees much of his dad." Johnny hopped over to Alex. "I'm not asking you to hang out with Jack every day. I just think it'd be nice to invite him to do something with us today on his birthday. That's all, just today."

Alex looked down while he thought. He let out a sigh. "All right."

Johnny's rabbit nose twitched, as it often did when he was happy.

"But just today," Alex cautioned. "What are we gonna do with a crow? I've never hung out with a bird before, let alone a crow. I don't think he'll like the same things that you and I do."

"Let's just ask Jack what he'd like to do. Who knows? We may learn a new game or something." Johnny looked at the pecans next to him. "Do we have enough yet?"

Alex checked their pile. "I think so. My mom always likes to gather pecans before the house family comes out to pick them up. She'll be so surprised that we did it for her!"

"How are we going to get these back to your tree?" asked Johnny.

"At times like this, I wish I was a chipmunk instead of a squirrel," said Alex. "Did you hear Munk bragging the other day about how he could carry *ten* acorns home in his mouth? I can only carry two in my mouth, at most. And these pecans are bigger than acorns." Alex looked around. "We need something that we could set all the pecans on and then just drag them home."

"What about one of the leaves that's fallen off the bigleaf magnolia tree? The tree near the house?"

"Perfect!" said Alex.

"Let's get the leaf, take these pecans to your mom, and then stop by the barn to ask Jack if he'd like to hang out with us."

Alex sighed. "All right. If we must."

"Come on, Alex," Johnny called as he hopped toward the house. "I think today could be the start of a great new friendship!"

"It'll definitely be the start of something . . ." Alex said to himself.

Alex was not looking forward to what the day would bring. But there was another animal who was dreading the day much more than Alex. As Johnny and Alex went to get the leaf, another conversation about the day's events was happening in the barn.

"Happy birthday, Jack!" said Cassie to her son.

"Thanks," Jack replied, emotionless. "I don't know how happy it's gonna be."

"Jack, I'm sure today will be a lot of fun!" Cassie said as she hobbled over, rolling an ear of corn to Jack.

"Corn *again*? It's my birthday, Mom. Can't I have an egg? I mean, the chicken coop is just next door. It would be so easy to get one."

"Jack!" Cassie looked around to make sure no one was listening. She whispered, "Jack, you know you can't say things like that. If the other animals heard you, they'd chase us out of this barn in a heartbeat."

"Good! I don't want to live in a barn! What crow lives in a barn?"

"Your mother, who cannot fly," Cassie said softly.

Jack hung his head.

Cassie wrapped her good wing around her son. "Jack, I know things haven't turned out for us like we planned, but we're so lucky that the barn animals accepted us and took us in. I couldn't have made it out in the fields. I wouldn't have survived."

"I know, Mom."

Cassie's voice perked up as she said, "But you know what? I became so much happier living here once I made some friends!"

"Aggh, Mom! Not more about the friend thing!"

"Jack, you left all your crow friends when you came to the barn with me. I just think you'd be much happier here if you made some new friends. I was talking to Bertha yesterday. You know her—she's the gray rabbit whose nest is near that big tree next to the fence. Anyway, she was telling me that her son, Johnny, is your age! And she mentioned his friend . . . What was his name? Started with an *A* . . . Adam? No. Alex! That's it, Alex. Anyway, I think you'd have a good time playing with them. What do you think?"

Jack sighed. "If I say yes, will you drop it about me making friends?"

Cassie smiled and held up her good wing. "I promise."

"Then . . . yeah. Fine. Whatever. I'll go hang out with a chubby ball of fur and a bushy-tailed rat. I can't even imagine what other crows would say if they saw me with a rabbit and a squirrel. If a crow sees us, I hope it thinks I'm just biding my time until I can eat one of them."

"Jack! You cannot say things like that! *Please!*"

CHAPTER 2

An Awkward Invitation

After Alex and Johnny delivered the surprise pecans to Alex's mom, they ran over to the barn to talk to Jack. When they went through the large double doors, they were greeted by the sweetest old voice. "Is that Alex and Johnny I see?" It was Ma Cow. Ma was like a grandmother to every animal on the farm.

"Yes, ma'am, Ma Cow. It's us," said Johnny as he hopped over to her stall door.

"How are you today, Ma?" Alex asked as he scurried up her door and sat on the lower half. This allowed Alex to be face-to-face with the large brown cow.

"Oh, I'm so glad to see you both. You boys sure are growin'. My, every time I see you two, you look more and more like your strong daddies."

Alex stuck his chest out, and Johnny wiggled his nose. They liked hearing that they were growing bigger. Ma had a way of making every young animal on the farm feel like they were her favorite.

"What brings you two fellas to the barn today?" Ma asked with a twinkle in her soft brown eyes.

"We've come to ask Jack the crow if he'd like to hang out with us. It's his birthday," Johnny answered.

"Now, boys, that is mighty nice of you to try and make that crow feel special on his birthday, but please be careful. I don't like sayin' anythang unkind, but I've been watchin' Jack for a while now, and he's . . . well, he's . . ." Ma struggled to find the right word because she really didn't like saying negative things about any of the animals, especially the young ones. She lowered her voice. "Well, to be honest, he's a *bad* crow."

"Yup, I've heard the same thing," said Alex.

"I've heard that too, but I'm hoping he's not really bad," said Johnny. "Maybe Jack's just confused or misunderstood. My mom told me he's had a rough time this year, with his mom getting hurt and all."

"Now that is true, yes it is, and I bet you are right. I just don't want you two sweet young'uns bein' influenced to be any different than you are. You see?"

"Oh, yes, ma'am. We promise, we won't do anything bad," answered Johnny. "Maybe if we show Jack how fun this farm is, he'll feel good about being here. I bet that'll make him act a lot better."

"Sweet, sweet Johnny, don't you ever change," said Ma.

Johnny's nose twitched. "Yes, ma'am." He looked at Alex. "You ready to go see Jack?"

Alex let out a breath of air. "I guess. Ma, next time we come by, could you tell us the story again about your son? The one who was in the rodeos? I love that story!"

Ma chuckled. "Absolutely, sugar. You sure do know how to make this old cow feel wanted."

"You're the best storyteller on the farm!" Alex said. Then he lowered his voice and leaned closer to Ma's ear. "But don't tell my mom I said that. See ya!" Alex scurried back down the doorframe as Johnny told Ma goodbye. The two friends headed to the back of the barn.

Ma laughed again and called after them, "Bye, boys! See you both soon!"

Johnny and Alex made their way down the barn's middle aisle. There was a hayloft above them where lots of hay was stored. The house dad also kept bales in the back corner stall. That's where Cassie and her son lived.

When Johnny and Alex got to the back stall, Johnny called out, "Hello? Mrs. Cassie? Jack?"

Cassie slowly came around the corner of a hay bale. She smiled when she saw them. "Oh, hello, boys! How are you both?"

"We're doing good," answered Johnny. "How are you?"

"I'm just fine. I'm so happy to see you two here! This is the perfect day for us to have visitors! It's my son Jack's birthday today! Jack?" She looked over behind another hay bale to her side. "Jack? Jack, come on out and speak to our company."

Jack emerged from behind the hay. He didn't speak. He just stared at Johnny and Alex.

"Hi, Jack. Happy birthday," said Johnny.

Jack said nothing.

Johnny looked at Alex.

"Oh yeah, happy birthday," Alex muttered.

They were met with silence once again and stared uncomfortably at each other. Finally,

Cassie said, "Johnny, how is your mom? She's such a sweet lady. I really do adore her!"

"She's doing good. She and my sisters are visiting my aunt today," Johnny answered.

"You have a lot of sisters, don't you? I tried to count them the other day when your mom and I were visiting, and I think I counted eight! Is that right?"

"Yes, ma'am," Johnny replied.

"Such a large, sweet family! I only have Jack, but I couldn't ask for a better son!" She looked over at Jack as he awkwardly stared at his feet. "Do you have any siblings, Alex?" Cassie asked, trying her best to keep the conversation going.

"I have two, a brother and a sister," answered Alex.

"Well, that's just great. Isn't that great, Jack?" Jack said nothing.

Cassie continued, "I've not met your mother yet, Alex, but I hope I'll get to soon." There was another uncomfortable silence, but Johnny broke the tension.

"Jack, we were wondering if you'd like to go do something with us." Johnny looked over at Mrs. Cassie and added, "If that's okay with you, ma'am?"

"Oh, I just think that is a wonderful idea! You three go out and have some fun playing together!

Doesn't that sound great, Jack?"

Jack said nothing.

Cassie went on, "Okay . . . well, you three just get going and have a marvelous time! And be careful!"

Jack didn't move.

Cassie added, "Jack, maybe when you get back, your dad will be here. I'm just sure he's going to come today to see the birthday boy!"

Jack finally hopped toward the door.

As he passed his mother, Cassie whispered, "Jack, please try. Please?"

CHAPTER 3

A Dangerous Proposal

The three boys silently made their way down the barn's center aisle, past Ma Cow's stall, and outside. As they stopped by the fence, Johnny asked, "Jack, since it's your birthday, what would you like to do? We're game for anything!"

Jack looked toward the woods. "I'm not sure if—"

"It speaks!" Alex shouted and then burst out laughing.

Johnny's nose twitched with amusement. Jack glared at Alex.

Alex swallowed down his laughter and said, "I'm sorry. I'm just kidding. What were you saying?"

Jack started again, "I'm not sure if you two are tough enough for what I have in mind."

Alex scowled at Jack.

"Well, let's hear it, and we'll see what we think," Johnny replied calmly.

Jack took three hops toward the woods. "I want to go find a snakeskin." He turned back to Johnny and Alex. "I know where a snake den is, and I think there may be a skin there."

"I'm sure there are lots of animal bones there too! And I don't want Johnny's or my bones added to the pile! No, thank you," Alex said emphatically. "Johnny, let's go do something else."

Jack chuckled smugly. "I knew you'd be too scared. Fine, I'll go by myself."

Just as Jack was about to take off flying, Johnny placed a paw on Jack's wing. "Wait. Jack, that really is dangerous. Why do you want a snakeskin?"

"That's none of your business!" Jack spat, shrugging Johnny's paw off.

22

Johnny stared at Jack, but not in an insulted or impatient way. Johnny's eyes were always very sincere. They showed concern.

After a few seconds, Jack said, "I want the snakeskin to show to my dad. Last time I saw him, he told me to go have lots of adventures and that he wanted to hear all about them the next time he came to visit. I think a snakeskin would be a pretty awesome thing to show him when he comes today."

"When was the last time you got to see your dad?" Johnny asked.

"You like the personal questions, don't you?" said Jack, irritated.

Johnny didn't answer.

After a few seconds, Jack looked off to the side and muttered, "About two months ago."

Johnny glanced at Alex and then back at Jack. "Okay, let's go," said Johnny.

"What?" Jack and Alex both said at the same time.

Johnny started hopping toward the woods. "Let's go get us a snakeskin!" He hollered back to them.

Alex and Jack looked at each other for a moment. Then Jack took off and flew after Johnny.

"I'm going to regret this," Alex muttered to himself before he scurried off after them.

The woods were about a half a mile from the barn. This wasn't a far distance for Jack to fly, but it was quite a trek for Johnny and Alex. When the boys made it to the edge of the woods, they stopped to catch their breath.

"So, where is the snake's den?" Johnny asked, breathing hard.

"There's a small creek about two miles into the woods," said Jack. "A spot near that creek has a bunch of big rocks. I was flying last week, just following the water, and I saw a copperhead curled up between some of the rocks. I think that would be a good place to find a skin."

"When do snakes molt? Is it the right time of year for that?" Johnny asked.

"Oh, snakes don't molt at a certain time of year," answered Alex. "Snakes shed their skin year-round and at different times from each other. We squirrels learn lots from watching things while we're up in the trees."

"I'll fly and lead the way," Jack said. "Just follow me."

"Sounds good, but we'll need to take a break every once in a while. I don't have wings," said Johnny.

Jack sighed. "Fine. I knew you two would just slow me down." Then Jack took off.

Alex and Johnny looked at each other.

"I don't think anyone misunderstands *that* crow," said Alex. The two friends ran into the woods, following as quickly as they could after Jack.

The woods grew thicker and darker the farther the trio went. After almost a mile, Jack landed on a rock and shouted back, "Guess you two need a break now. You're slowing down a lot. I'd already be there if I was alone."

"Jack, how about you hop on your legs with us and see how fast *you* go?" Alex said as he sat down.

Johnny plopped down next to Alex and said, "Alex, when we get going again, why don't you go up a tree and jump branches? I know that's quicker for you. Not to mention much safer too."

"I'm not leaving you down on the ground by yourself, Johnny. No, it's fine."

The three boys sat quietly for a minute and rested. Johnny broke the silence by saying, "Alex, didn't your dad kill a snake once?"

"Yeah, it wasn't a super big one, but he sure did. Then he ate it! My dad's pretty much the bravest squirrel on the farm," Alex boasted.

"Brave for a squirrel," muttered Jack.

"What's *that* supposed to mean?" Alex stood up, squaring his shoulders.

"Just what I said. I'm sure your dad is brave for a squirrel, but that's nothing compared to how brave crows are. *My* dad has killed more snakes than I can even count."

Sensing a fight was about to break out, Johnny quickly said, "Well, I think it's a good time for you to lead on, Jack." Johnny stood up. "Just let me get a good stretch first."

Johnny stretched his back and then turned his head as far as it would go to the left and to the right. As Johnny stretched to the right, he gasped. "Jack! Look! I can't believe it!"

CHAPTER 4

A Success and a Loss

Johnny hopped over and picked up a gigantic snakeskin next to a pile of leaves. He held it out for Jack and Alex to see. "How lucky are we?"

"Johnny! Move!" screamed Alex just as a black kingsnake shot out of the leaf pile.

Thankfully, Johnny was about a foot farther than the snake's strike could reach. Alex dashed over to Johnny and shoved him out of the way just before the snake could strike again. Johnny rolled like a ball into the pile of leaves. The snake quickly turned back and slithered after Johnny. Alex jumped onto the snake just behind its head and bit down hard.

Jack stood frozen, watching the absolute chaos in front of him. The snake tried to wrap its tail around Alex's chest. Johnny, snakeskin still in his paws, jumped out of the leaves and kicked with all of his might at the snake's midsection. Alex kept biting the snake over and over. Because of Johnny's kicks and Alex's bites, the snake had not yet been able to wrap its tail around Alex. The snake turned toward Johnny to strike again.

Jack shook his head to break his trance and flew over to the fight. "Move, Johnny!" Jack yelled as he grabbed the snake's tail with his claws. Johnny jumped back into the pile of leaves. Jack tried to pull the snake's tail away from Alex, but the snake was too large for Jack to pick up completely. Managing to drag the snake about two feet away from the leaf pile, Jack shouted, "Jump off, Alex!"

Alex sprang headfirst into the pile of leaves.

Before letting go of the snake, Jack bent down and pecked at the snake's tail as hard as he could. He watched the snake slither quickly into the bushes. Jack didn't look away until the snake had completely disappeared.

Alex and Johnny poked their heads out of the leaf pile.

"Let's get out of here!" Jack yelled. He took off flying, heading back toward the barn.

Johnny and Alex jumped out of the leaves and ran as fast as they could go, following Jack.

They didn't stop until they were out of the woods and back to the fenced-in meadow. When they cleared the trees, Alex and Johnny fell down to rest. Jack landed next to them. All three were gasping for air.

Johnny sat up and took the rolled-up snakeskin from his mouth. "Success!" he said as he held it up.

"What?" Jack asked in disbelief. "You held on to it through all of that?"

"Yeah," said Johnny, still breathing hard. He handed the skin to Jack. "It was important to you, so I held on to it."

Jack stared wide-eyed at Johnny. Jack had never had anyone other than his mom do something nice for him. He didn't know how to act now. Jack took the snakeskin from Johnny and quietly said, "Thanks."

"It has manners?" Alex asked sarcastically.

29

But his voice didn't sound confrontational like it had been before when he spoke to Jack. Alex's voice sounded lighthearted and teasing.

Jack looked mischievously at Alex. "Don't get used to it, squirrel."

And there they were. Friends. The snake battle had accomplished what Cassie could never have done.

As they headed back to the barn, Jack said, "When did you roll this thing up, Johnny?"

"While I was running like crazy, and that was *not* easy. I just didn't want it to get snagged on something and break off. I think your dad will be shocked at how long the snakeskin is."

"I can't wait to show him," said Jack.

"And I can't wait to tell *my* dad about it," Alex said as they reached the barn doors. "That snake was, like, three times longer than the one he ate!"

"Well, I better get home," said Johnny. "My mom will be wondering where I'm at. Happy birthday, Jack."

"Yeah, happy birthday," echoed Alex.

"Thanks," said Jack awkwardly. He hadn't used that word much, and it felt weird for him to say. Carrying the snakeskin, Jack headed into the barn as Alex and Johnny ran to their homes. Jack was in too much of a hurry to hop, so he flew to the back stall.

"Dad?" Jack called as he flew through the stall door. No answer. He landed and said again, "Dad?"

Cassie slowly hobbled around one of the hay bales. Her head was down. "Jack, Dad's not here." She looked up at him. "But the sun hasn't gone down completely yet, so maybe he's still on his way."

Jack dropped the snakeskin to the floor and looked down. "Yeah, maybe."

CHAPTER 5

Your Worst Nightmare

Cassie saw the snakeskin at Jack's feet. "Jack! Where on earth did you get that? You didn't mess with a snake, did you? Jack! Where are those nice boys? Johnny and Alex? Did a snake eat them?"

"Mom, they're fine." Jack picked up the snakeskin and hopped past his mother. He didn't want to talk about anything. He just wanted to be alone.

Cassie followed him to the back wall. "Jack, look at what I found outside today." She limped over to the base of the wall, and using her beak, pulled something out from the crack between the wall and the floor. She dropped it at Jack's feet. "Look! Isn't it wonderful?"

Jack looked down to see a small round shiny coin. "Great," he said halfheartedly.

"Ma Cow told me that people call this a dime. I used my wing feathers and shined it up so nicely. Don't you think?" Cassie was trying to look into her son's eyes, but Jack was still staring at the floor. "You can have it, Jack. That might make you feel better? Hmm? You could show it to your dad when he gets here and—"

"He's not coming, Mom!" Jack burst out. He looked down again and quietly added, "He doesn't care."

Cassie hobbled over to Jack and put her wing around him. She spoke softly. "Jack, I know you're sad and disappointed that he isn't here. I am too. But your father loves you."

Jack pulled away from her.

Cassie continued, "I just have to believe that something must have come up that kept him from coming today."

"We haven't seen him in forever, Mom. He used to come see us every other day, then it was every week, then every two weeks . . . It's been almost two months now." Jack turned his back to his mother. "He just doesn't care about me anymore."

"No, Jack, no. Your father loves you, and I know he misses you. It's just . . . well, he doesn't want to be a part of this barn life."

"Neither do I," Jack muttered. He quickly turned to see tears welling up in Cassie's eyes.

Cassie swallowed. "I know you don't, Jack." Her head dropped. "You can go back to the fields with your father. You can, Jack. You don't have to stay here with me. I'll be fine on my own. But I'll . . . I . . ." She started to cry. "I sure would miss you, son."

Jack hopped over to her. "Mom, I'm sorry. I didn't mean it. I don't want to leave you. I'd never leave you." The two crows put the tops of their heads together.

Jack could not stand to see his mom cry. He didn't care about many things, but Jack secretly adored his mother. Oh, she annoyed him with her constant talking and her obsession with shiny objects, but Jack knew no one in the world loved him like Cassie did. He also knew how much she needed him.

Cassie wiped her eyes with her good wing, sniffed, and said, "Well, did you have fun with Johnny and Alex?"

34

"Yeah . . . I did."

"Oh, I'm so glad, Jack! Are they nice boys? What all did you three do today? Where all did you go? Did they—"

"Mom," Jack interrupted, "they're okay. I think I'm gonna go to bed now."

"Oh, I bet you're worn out from your big day! I'm going to stay up for a little bit and look through my collection, but you go on to bed. I love you, birthday boy!"

"Love you," Jack replied as he hopped off to bed.

The next morning, Jack was pecking the ground for bugs near the big tree by the fence. "What are you doing here, crow?" a playful voice asked. Jack looked up to see Alex coming his way.

"I'm searching for bugs, squirrel. That okay with you?"

"Ahhh, bugs. The breakfast of champions. You waiting to see Johnny?" Alex asked as he sat down next to Jack.

"What? No, does he live here?" Jack pretended to not know, but he'd chosen that spot to hunt for insects because he knew it was near Johnny's nest. Jack secretly hoped he'd run into Johnny and Alex and they'd invite him to hang out with them again.

"Yeah, he lives over there," Alex answered as he nodded toward the big tree.

When they both looked at the tree, Johnny popped out of his nest. He saw them and hopped over.

"Hey, guys! What's up?" Johnny greeted them.

"Ahhh, nothing," answered Alex. "Crow boy here was just hunting some bugs."

"What'd your dad think of that snakeskin?" Johnny asked Jack.

Jack looked down and shifted back and forth. "He couldn't make it yesterday." He looked over at Alex. "He was probably stealing food from an eagle or doing something dangerous like that and lost track of time."

"I'm sorry he didn't make it," said Johnny.

Jack looked off toward the barn. "Oh, I don't care. What are you guys doing today?"

"Johnny! Johnny?" a voice called.

The boys turned toward Johnny's nest to see his mother's head sticking out. "Johnny, come here, dear. I need your help for a minute."

"Coming!" Johnny called to his mom. He looked at the boys and said, "Be right back."

Johnny hopped over to his nest.

Alex and Jack waited in silence for a minute before Jack said, "That Johnny, does he ask everyone lots of personal questions?"

"Yeah, but it's just 'cause he cares. He's a nice guy, a great friend. And other than my dad, Johnny is the bravest animal I've ever met. If you're ever in a scary spot, you want that rabbit with you."

Johnny came out of his nest and hopped back over to the boys. "Sorry about that. So, what should we three do today?"

Jack was thrilled that he was being included, but he made sure his face didn't show it.

"What day is it? Is it Saturday?" asked Alex.

"It is! It's Saturday!" Johnny answered.

"School day!" Johnny and Alex both shouted excitedly.

"School day? What's that?" asked Jack.

"Madelyn teaches all the animals school on Saturdays. It's awesome!" said Alex.

"Who's Madelyn?" Jack asked.

Just then, they heard the ringing of a bell.

"Oh! It's school time! Come on, we'll tell you on the way," said Johnny. The three headed toward the house. "Madelyn is the daughter of the house family," Johnny continued.

Jack stopped in his tracks. "Human! She's a

human? I'm not going around humans!"

"She's not dangerous, Jack. No one in the house family is. And besides, we're not going right up to her. We're just getting close enough to hear and see her," said Johnny.

They started moving again. "Yeah, we can't go right up to her even if we wanted to because of Bridgett," added Alex.

"Who's Bridgett?" asked Jack.

"Your worst nightmare," Alex said coldly.

"Bridgett is the teacher's pet," Johnny explained. "She's the house cat, and she's evil."

"Oh, that fat gray-and-white cat?" said Jack. "I've seen her around a little but not much."

"That's because she mainly stays in the house, but sometimes she comes out with Madelyn and Derek," said Johnny.

"Who's Derek?" asked Jack.

"He's the house family's son—Madelyn's brother," answered Johnny.

"I've seen those kids playing outside, but I didn't know their names. What makes that Bridgett so evil?" asked Jack.

"She killed and ate my uncle," said Alex.

CHAPTER 6

Schooltime

"Normally, a cat could never catch a squirrel. We're much too fast for them," Alex boasted. "But one day, my uncle jumped onto a rotten branch, and it broke off of the tree. He fell to the ground, and a limb landed on his head. Knocked him right out.

"That beast cat was outside with the house kids. Madelyn came over to see what had happened, and I bet she would have tried to help him. But before she could, that devil cat snatched him up and carried him away. The next day, my dad found my uncle's tail behind the barn. That was all that was left of him . . . just his tail."

The three were quiet for a minute as Johnny and Jack processed what Alex had just shared. When the boys reached the fence between the barn and the house, they hid behind a post.

"We'll wait here to make sure Bridgett isn't with the house kids," whispered Johnny. "Madelyn usually locks that cat inside the house. She knows none of us smaller animals will come to school if Bridgett's outside."

There was a wooden picnic table in the backyard, close to the fence. They watched as Madelyn propped a small chalkboard up against a bucket on top of the table. Derek was marching around the yard. Madelyn grabbed her little bell and shook it again. "Schooltime!" Madelyn yelled. "Derek, come over here and be my teaching assistant."

"I want to play army!" Derek called back.

"What kind of stuff does she teach during schooltime?" Jack whispered.

"All sorts of things," answered Johnny. "Last week, she taught us about a holiday called Thanksgiving."

"You and your mom have been here for a few months, Jack. How come you've never heard Madelyn calling for school or been to any of the classes?" asked Alex.

"I usually head to the woods or out to the cornfields as soon as daylight comes. I haven't really liked staying around the barn."

"Do you go visit your dad?" Johnny asked.

"I don't want to talk about my dad!" Jack snapped. "I mean . . ." Jack shifted back and forth on his feet. "I don't like to leave my mom all alone. So no."

They heard Madelyn's bell ring again. The barn doors were open, and Alex saw Ma Cow slowly coming out.

"Here comes Ma for school. I was wondering where she was," said Alex.

Ma came over to the fence where the boys were hiding behind the post.

"Hi, Ma Cow!" said Johnny.

"We were wondering where you were," added Alex.

"Oh, you know me, boys. I'm gettin' old and movin' pretty slow. It takes me a bit to get goin' these days. Has she started the lesson yet?"

"No, ma'am, but she's just about to," answered Johnny.

Jack looked around to see who all was in attendance. There were two horses at the fence down a bit from them. He saw four goats on the other side of the horses. Something moving toward the picnic table caught Jack's eye. He looked to see a golden retriever coming. "Do you two need to worry about that dog?"

"Nah, that's Honey. She's as old as mud," answered Alex.

"Honey is a sweet, sweet dog," said Ma. "She used to love to chase animals when she was young, but now she's like me and would rather rest than run around."

Honey lay down next to the picnic table. Her golden fur was all white on her face.

"Now, class," Madelyn began, "last week we learned about the pilgrims, the *Mayflower*, and how we eat a huge meal and think about what we're thankful for. Today's lesson is about another awesome holiday, and that's Christmas." Madelyn turned to Derek, who was now pretending that the back porch steps were his helicopter. "Derek! Come tell the class about Santa with me!"

"I don't want to! I'm still playing army!" Derek yelled back.

Madelyn let out a disappointed sigh and

turned back to the animals. "I'm sorry, class. My assistant can't be with us today. He's been drafted to fight in a war. Now, back to our lesson. Yesterday, Derek and I put something very special into the mailbox. Does anyone know what that was? Raise your hand if you know." She looked around the animals and then went on. "Yesterday, we mailed our Santa letters!" As Madelyn spoke, she wrote "Santa Letters" on her chalkboard.

Madelyn went on to teach the animals all about who Santa Claus was. She told them that every year on the day after Thanksgiving, she and Derek write Santa letters and put them in the mailbox.

"Mom and Dad always tell us that we can ask Santa for three things: something big, something medium, and something small. I asked him for a bike, a princess tent, and an art set. Derek asked him for a telescope, this race car-set thing, and . . ." She turned back to Derek. "Derek, you asked for a telescope, race car set, and what was the third thing?"

"A marble tower!" Derek answered.

Madelyn turned back to the animals. "That's right, a marble tower. And Santa also brings lots of little gifts to put into our stockings. But you have to be as good as you can be all year long for

Santa to bring you gifts. He won't bring anything if you're bad. Okay, class, that's all for today's lesson. Next week, I'll bring out our nativity set, and I'll teach you the true meaning of Christmas. Class is dismissed!"

"I wish there was a Santa for animals!" Alex said as they watched Madelyn gather up her chalkboard, bucket, and chalk.

"Wouldn't change anything for me if there was one," said Jack. "I probably wouldn't get any gifts."

"I'm glad you said it, 'cause I was thinking it!" Alex laughed.

Jack glared at Alex.

"Now, Jack, you could be good if you wanted to be," said Johnny.

"I guess that's the thing." Jack grinned. "Do I want to be?"

CHAPTER 7

The Christmas Tree

The week went by very quickly. The animals had lots of entertainment to watch as the house family decorated for Christmas. One day, the house dad placed white lights all along the roofline of their home. The next day, the house mom hung wreaths on the front and back doors.

A couple of days after that, the house family went out into the woods. The house dad was carrying a saw. They were gone for almost an hour. When they emerged from the woods, the house dad was pulling a tree behind him. He took the tree right inside their house!

Soon, it was Saturday again. The animals gathered at the fence for school. It was a cold day, but they didn't want to miss the next lesson. Madelyn rang her bell and announced, "Students! It's time for school!"

Derek and Madelyn both had on their hats, coats, and gloves. They were sitting on opposite sides of the picnic table with a box on top of the table between them.

"Class, today we are going to teach y'all about the nativity and the night that Jesus was born in Bethlehem. I'm going to tell you about each person in the story, and as I do, Derek will hold up their nativity piece for you to see. And there are even animals in the story! You're all gonna love it!"

Madelyn told the Christmas story to the animals as Derek held up each wooden figurine. At the end of the lesson, Madelyn and Derek arranged the nativity set on the picnic table.

"We'd leave this here for y'all to enjoy, but Mom told us we had to bring it back inside when we're done," Madelyn said. "Mom likes it set up on our coffee table in the family room."

As Madelyn and Derek placed the nativity pieces back into the box, Madelyn said, "Derek, would you like to tell the class what we'll be teaching them next Saturday?"

"Oh yes," Derek replied in a very grown-up-sounding voice. "Next Saturday, we'll teach you all about Christmas trees." Then he whispered to Madelyn, "Can I dismiss class today?" Madelyn nodded. "Class is dismissed!" Derek announced.

"I love school," Alex sighed.

"Yeah, it's really interesting," said Johnny.

They both looked at Jack.

Jack shrugged his wings. "It's okay."

"Want to go over to the pond and see if it's frozen yet?" Alex asked them.

"I can't," Jack answered. "My mom wasn't feeling good this morning—the cold makes her foot and wing ache. She said she didn't feel up to getting her food for the day, so she asked me to go find her some lunch once school was over."

"We can help you," Johnny offered.

"Nah, I can do it. I'm going to fly to find her something, so that would make it hard for us to stay together."

"Okay. Well, see you later," said Johnny.

"See ya," said Jack as he flew away.

When Jack was out of sight, Alex asked, "How did Mrs. Cassie hurt her foot and wing?"

"I'm not sure," Johnny replied. "My mom told me that Mrs. Cassie had a terrible accident a few months ago. Mom said that the house mom saved Mrs. Cassie's life. I didn't get a chance to ask Mom more about it 'cause my sister started choking on a carrot. Mom got her to cough it up, but it was scary."

The following Saturday, Madelyn and Derek brought out a larger box than they had the previous week. They set it on the picnic table. Madelyn rang her little bell and called out, "Schooltime!" As Madelyn and Derek sat down at the table, the usual animals took their places at the fence.

"Hello, class! First, I have a wonderful announcement! Derek's and my last day of real school is on Friday, so after that, we'll be home every day for almost three weeks!"

"What's *real* school?" Alex whispered to Johnny.

"I'm not sure," Johnny whispered back.

Madelyn stood and picked up the box. "For today's lesson, we're going to teach you about Christmas trees, and as we talk, we're actually going to decorate a tree for you!"

She carried the box over to a young maple tree about twenty feet from the picnic table. The tree was just a tiny bit taller than Madelyn and had no leaves.

"Now, this is not the right kind of tree to decorate as a Christmas tree, but this is what we're going to use for our demonstration," Madelyn explained.

"And Mom said we can leave it decorated!" added Derek.

"Yes, so y'all can enjoy it until after Christmas Day," said Madelyn as she set the box on the ground next to the tree.

The animals watched as the house kids hung ornaments all over the bare branches. As Derek hung the last ornament, Madelyn reached up and placed a shiny metal star on top of the tallest middle branch.

"Oh no," said Jack.

CHAPTER 8

What Happened to Cassie

"What's wrong?" asked Alex.

"I hope my mom doesn't see that star," said Jack. "I'm going to have problems if she does."

"Why would that be a problem?" Johnny asked.

"My mom is obsessed with shiny things . . .

like, *obsessed.* It's how we got stuck here."

Johnny and Alex didn't speak. They stood staring at Jack, waiting for him to continue.

"My mom loves anything that shines. She collects shiny things. Earlier this year, she was flying around, looking for stuff to add to her collection. She flew by this house, and something on the porch caught her eye. It made bell noises when the wind blew."

"A wind chime," Johnny interjected.

"Well, Mom just *had* to have that wind chime. She grabbed ahold of it with her feet. She pulled and pulled, but it wouldn't come off the porch's ceiling. So she put some of the strings in her beak and held on to the other strings with her feet. She gave it a good yank. It came out of the ceiling, but it was much heavier than Mom expected. She fell down on the porch. The . . . What was it called again?"

"Wind chime," answered Johnny.

"The wind chime landed on top of her. Mom wasn't hurt, but she was wrapped up in the strings."

"So how did she get hurt, then?" asked Alex.

"I guess the wind chime falling made a lot of noise. The house mom came out on the porch and saw Mom caught in the strings. Mom was afraid that the house mom was going to hurt her, so

51

Mom went crazy trying to get loose."

"The house mom would never have hurt Mrs. Cassie," said Johnny. "I'm sure the house mom was just gonna try to help free your mom."

"Well, she scared Mom so badly that Mom wiggled right off of the porch. She landed hard on some bricks. When she fell, one of the strings got caught on the porch, and that string was wrapped around Mom's wing. The string cut into her wing, and when she landed, she broke one of her feet."

"What did the house mom do?" asked Alex.

"She put her apron over Mom's head—I guess so Mom wouldn't try to peck at her. Then she freed Mom from the strings. Mom told me that the house dad came out and asked what was going on. The house mom told him that a crow had gotten hurt. He told her to just let Bridgett have the bird! I didn't know who Bridgett was then, but I do now. The house mom said she couldn't do that. He told her she should because that would be one less crow eating up the vegetables, but she didn't listen to him.

"She carried Mom to the barn and laid her on top of one of the hay bales in the back stall— where we live now. She brought Mom food and water every day until Mom was strong enough to get around."

"How'd you find your mom?" asked Johnny. "I mean, after she got hurt, how did you know she was here?"

"Mom said that on her first night, the barn owl came into her stall."

"Mr. Archie?" Alex asked.

"Yes. Mom was terrified. You know, some owls eat crows. But he told Mom to not be scared because he'd eaten a crow once when he was young and gotten really sick from it. He said he'd never eat crow again."

"You're lucky *you* don't have to worry about Mr. Archie. We can't go out much at night because of him. He loves rabbits and squirrels," said Alex.

"What happened next?" asked Johnny.

"Mom begged Archie to be on the lookout for her husband and son because she was sure we'd be searching for her. She asked Archie that if he saw crows flying around here, to let them know that she was inside the barn."

"Class is dismissed!" called out Madelyn. The boys had completely forgotten about the Christmas tree lesson.

"Anyway, when Mom didn't come home that night, I knew something was wrong. Dad said she was probably fine, that she'd most likely found some heavy shiny thing and was dragging it home. But I just had a feeling that something bad had happened. I went out searching for her that morning. I flew all day. The sun had set by the time I got to this farm. As I was flying between the house and the barn, I heard, 'Cassie is in the barn!' I looked in the direction of the voice and saw a huge owl sitting on the barn's roof. I yelled back, 'How do I know you're telling me the truth?' I didn't know if it was a trick so he could try to eat me or what. My mom heard me and called out my name. I flew in one of the barn windows and found her."

"And you decided to stay with her," said Johnny.

"I stayed for the rest of that night, and then I flew back to the fields the next morning to tell my dad. He came back with me to check on her. She was in bad shape. Dad said he thought it would be a good idea if I stayed to help her. He said he'd come see us every other day until she was healed enough to fly back home to the fields."

Jack looked down. "After a few weeks, it was pretty obvious that Mom would never fly again." Jack took a deep breath and let it out. "She needs me." He looked at Johnny and Alex. "So I stayed."

CHAPTER 9

Mind Your Own Business

Jack, Johnny, and Alex turned their attention back to Madelyn and Derek, who were admiring the yard's beautiful and unique Christmas tree.

"Derek, go in the house and get an apple, please," said Madelyn.

"Are you hungry?"

"Not for me! Remember? It's Jasper's birthday today!"

"Oh yeah!" Derek said as he turned and ran to the house. Jasper was their dad's horse, and Jasper *loved* apples.

"The barn animals get the best treats!" said Alex.

"Not *all* the barn animals," added Jack.

Johnny looked at the animals along the fence and said, "Jasper isn't here today."

Derek came out the back door and jumped off the porch. "I got the apple, but Mom said that Dad rode Jasper over to the Haynies' house."

"Let's just set the apple on Jasper's stall door. Dad can give it to Jasper when they get back," said Madelyn. "I'm afraid we'll forget to take it to him if we wait until later." Madelyn and Derek ran to the barn.

"Well, I better get home and see what's for lunch. I'm hungry," said Alex.

"I am too. See you guys later?" asked Johnny.

"Sure," said Alex as Jack nodded.

The three went in different directions, with Jack heading back to the barn. He waited behind one of the barn doors while the kids delivered the apple. After a couple of minutes, Jack whispered, "What's taking those two so long?" He peeked through a crack in the door and saw

Madelyn petting Ma Cow on the neck.

Madelyn said, "You are the sweetest cow ever! See ya later, Ma Cow!"

Jack hid behind the door as Madelyn and Derek left. As soon as they were past the fence, Jack hopped into the barn. He went to Jasper's stall, which was across the aisle from Ma Cow's. Jack flew up and sat next to the apple. As he bit the stem with his beak, he heard someone say, "Jack." He let go of the stem and turned to see Ma Cow staring at him and shaking her head.

"That apple is *not* yours," Ma said sternly.

"I've been eating only bugs and corn for weeks. I'm taking this, and you can't stop me."

"Now, son . . ." Ma started.

"Mind your own business! And I'm not *your* son." With that, Jack picked up the apple by the stem and flew to his and Cassie's stall. Jack landed beside one of the many hay bales in the room. He carefully set the apple on the floor. "Mom? You here?"

Cassie slowly limped around one of the bales. She had a silver gum wrapper in her beak. Cassie dropped the wrapper when she saw the apple. "Jack, where did you get that?"

"I was sitting in a tree, and the house son came outside with this apple. I heard him tell his sister that he thought the apple had a worm in it. Then

57

he threw it out into the field. I went and got it for you!" Jack was a very quick and believable liar.

"Oh my goodness! What a treat! Oh! I hope it *does* have a worm in it! That would be two treats!" Cassie hobbled over to Jack and hugged him. "You're so good to me, son. Thank you." She backed up and admired the large red apple. "But this apple is much too big for just me! Would you share it with me?"

"Sure," Jack answered. He knew his mom would always share anything she had with him. She always did.

As they were eating, Cassie asked, "So how has your day been so far?"

"Fine."

"My day has been wonderful too! Not only did my sweet son bring me this delicious lunch, but I went out this morning just to have a quick look around, and look at what I found!" She nodded over to the empty gum wrapper lying on the floor. "Isn't it great?"

"Great," Jack said while he chewed.

"I was just about to hide it with everything else in my collection when you came in. I have to hide it all so no one will steal it."

"Mom, no one is ever going to steal your junk."

"It's not junk. It's my beautiful collection." Cassie looked down at the piece of apple in her good wing. "My collection makes me happy," she said softly.

Jack stared at his mom. "I know," he said thoughtfully. He looked over at the wrapper. "You know, that wrapper is pretty special. You may need to go ahead and hide it before anyone sees it. I bet they *would* try to steal it."

Cassie immediately perked up. "You think so? I mean, it is very special, isn't it?" She set her part of the apple down and limped over to the wrapper. "I'll just go hide this right now. Please watch the door, Jack." Cassie hobbled over to the wall behind one of the hay bales. There, she shoved the wrapper into the crack where the wall and the floor met. This was where Cassie hid her shiny keepsakes.

"Jack, I'm going to be out for a bit after you go to bed tonight," Cassie said as she shuffled back over to her piece of the apple.

"Not tonight, Mom. It's cold, and you never know what animals are out and about. You can't fly away from danger."

"I know that, son, but I'll be careful, like I always am. I want to see if the house family has set out any more shiny Christmas decorations. Maybe I'll find some small things for my collection!"

Jack remembered the metal star on top of

Madelyn and Derek's Christmas tree. "No, Mom, I really think you should stay in tonight. Maybe we could . . ." He looked around. ". . . pull all of your collection out and shine them up?"

"As fun as that does sound, we can do that in the morning. I don't want to wait and miss out on the pickings!" Cassie said as she ate.

"Mom, no other animal on this farm cares about shiny things—just you."

"You think that, Jack, but I guarantee you lots of other animals here have good taste, too, and have their own hidden collections."

Jack rolled his eyes.

CHAPTER 10

Wisdom from Archie

When bedtime came, Cassie hugged Jack good-night and started on her journey to the yard. The trek took her quite a while. Jack used that time to fly out one of the windows and up to the barn's roof. From there, he could watch Cassie down below and make sure she was safe. This was what Jack always did when his mom was out late hunting treasures—unbeknownst to Cassie.

The house dad closed the barn doors every night, so Cassie needed help getting out of the barn. When she got to Ma's stall, Cassie whispered, "Mrs. Ma Cow, are you awake?"

Ma raised her head over the top of her door. "I sure am, dear. Are you needin' some fresh air this cool night, Mrs. Cassie?"

"Yes, ma'am. Could you please help me again? If you don't mind?"

"Don't mind at all, sugar!" Ma Cow bit the latch on her stall door and slid it to the right. She pushed against her door, and it swung open. Ma slowly walked to the barn's large sliding doors. She grabbed one of the handles with her teeth and pulled it just a few inches to the side, making an opening wide enough for Cassie to go through. "Let me know when you're back inside, and I'll come close the door. And you be careful, Mrs. Cassie."

"Oh, I'll be careful. Thank you!" Cassie shuffled through the doors and turned left. She headed toward the house when something she saw made her stop—Madelyn and Derek's Christmas tree.

Jack watched from above as his mother limped over to the tree. For a couple of minutes, Cassie stood just staring up at the shiny metal star on top. Jack knew his mom was trying to figure out how she could get that star. Jack's attention was broken when something large landed next to him. He turned to see Mr. Archie.

"She's out again tonight?" Archie asked. Jack nodded. "I figured all these decorations would be too tempting for her. It's dangerous for your mother out here at night. Birds aren't safe on the ground, and she moves so slowly, she'd never get away from a predator."

"That's why I'm here," Jack replied as he watched his mom.

"Jack, you can't protect your mother from everything, especially from herself. When someone refuses to learn from a mistake, they're bound to make it again. If the wind chime incident didn't cure your mother of this foolish fixation, most likely, nothing will."

Jack wanted to tell Archie to mind his own business, but Archie's size and physical closeness kept Jack quiet. They sat silently, watching Cassie hobble over to a low-hanging branch. She pulled off a plastic, glittery icicle ornament.

With her treasure in her beak, Cassie headed toward the barn doors. Jack waited until she was safely in the barn. Then, without a word to Archie, Jack took off and flew inside one of the barn windows.

The next morning, Cassie showed Jack her newest trinket. She held the icicle ornament up with her good wing. "Isn't it beautiful, Jack?"

"Beautiful," Jack said without even looking.

"There were so many sparkling things all over a tree in the yard! At the very top, there was a gorgeous star. I wanted it so badly! But I couldn't get it, so I chose this instead. Not as big or beautiful as the star but still lovely. I'm going to go hide this right now."

Cassie limped over to the back wall and pushed the ornament into the crack above the floor. "My collection is really growing! Maybe tonight, you and I could pull everything out and look through it? That would be fun! Wouldn't it?"

Jack sighed. "Yep."

"Do you have plans with your friends today?" Cassie asked.

"Alex likes to go over to the pond to see if it's frozen yet. We may do that."

"Those boys are both so nice. I'm glad you've found some great friends, Jack. They've made being here at the barn better for you . . . right?" Cassie asked hopefully.

"Yeah, I guess so. I mean, it's a lot less boring than it used to be."

"Oh, I'm so happy, Jack!" Cassie shuffled over and hugged him. "I could never be happy if you weren't, son."

CHAPTER 11

Cassie's Idea

The Saturday before Christmas was another chilly day. Madelyn and Derek sat side by side on top of the picnic table. They both had their knees pulled up to their chins.

"Class, this Wednesday is Christmas Day!" said Madelyn.

"And this Tuesday is Christmas Eve!" added Derek. "Christmas Eve is almost as much fun as Christmas Day!"

"It really is," Madelyn agreed. "On Tuesday, our grandparents, aunts, uncles, and cousins are all coming over here for lunch. Last year, we all went to Aunt Manda's house. So this year, it's our turn to have everyone come here."

"And after we eat, we open presents!" said Derek.

"Yes! And after we open presents, Grandpa, Dad, and Uncle Adrian will take naps while us kids all play with our new toys. Then we'll eat the lunch leftovers for dinner. After that, we're gonna do something so fun! It's the first time we've ever done this on Christmas Eve, and it was my and Derek's idea! We're going to . . ." Madelyn looked over at Derek and whispered, "Derek, you tell them the big news."

"Oh, okay! We're going to have a huge bonfire out here! We asked Dad if we could, and he said yes!"

"And we're going to drink hot chocolate and make s'mores and sing carols . . . It's going to be awesome!" Madelyn said.

"I don't like s'mores. I'm just gonna eat the chocolate bars," said Derek.

"After that, everyone will go home, and we'll get

ready for bed. We'll get in our pajamas and leave milk and cookies out for Santa. It's how you thank Santa for your gifts—you leave him a snack. Then Dad reads us the Christmas story from the Bible."

"And then we go to bed so Santa can come! I think he'll get to our house at one a.m.," Derek said as he pulled his hat down over his ears. "Madelyn, I'm cold. Can we end school now and go inside?"

"Sure, I'm cold too." Turning to the animals, Madelyn announced, "Class is dismissed."

According to Madelyn and Derek, Christmas Eve took *forever* to come. But finally, Tuesday morning found the kids and their dad outside preparing for the day.

All the animals on the farm called Madelyn and Derek's parents "the house dad" and "the house mom," but the kids' parents of course had real names. Their dad's name was Jim, and their mom's name was Iva Jo.

Madelyn and Derek collected sticks for the bonfire while Jim set chairs around the firepit.

Excitement was in the air! So much so that even the animals could feel it! Most of them were watching the kids and their dad as they worked. Johnny, Alex, and Jack watched and listened from behind a tree.

"Dad, are you sure it won't rain during the bonfire?" asked Madelyn. "The sky looks pretty gray."

"Shouldn't start raining until tonight, around eleven or after, so I think we'll be fine. Derek, go grab me two buckets out of the barn, please," Jim said as he set out the last chair.

"Sure, Dad." Derek ran to the barn while Madelyn brought another armload of sticks to a pile beside the firepit.

"Dad, thank you for letting us have the bonfire tonight!" said Madelyn as she dropped the sticks onto the pile.

"You're welcome, sweetie. This'll be a lot of fun. It'll be cold, but we'll all bundle up. And the fire will help."

"And the hot chocolate!" added Madelyn.

"Here, Dad," Derek said, breathing hard as he handed Jim the two buckets.

"Thanks, bud. You two keep gathering sticks. I'll be right back." Jim walked over to the side of the house.

After a couple of minutes, Jim came back with

the buckets filled with water. He set them down near the firepit.

"What are those for, Dad?" asked Derek.

"We'll pour the water on the fire to put it out when we're done tonight."

"Won't that water freeze out here?" asked Madelyn.

"No, it'll be cold, but the low is supposed to only be around forty degrees," Jim answered.

"Can *we* pour the water on the fire tonight, Dad? Please?" Derek asked.

"Oh, yes, please?" added Madelyn.

"Sure. But you'll both have to be very careful. Don't get too close to the fire, and make sure you cover it completely with the water. I'll be here to help if you need me."

Jack had enough of watching Madelyn and Derek interact with their dad. He felt hot tears coming to his eyes, but he could *not* let Johnny and Alex see. Jack turned his back to the boys as he looked at the barn. He lied and said, "I just heard my mom call me. I'll see you guys later." Jack flew as fast as he could to the barn.

Jack didn't stop until he was in his and Cassie's stall. He sat down and wiped his eyes with his wings.

"Jack? Jack, honey? Is that you?" Cassie said from behind the hay bales.

"Oh, yeah, it's me," Jack said as he got himself back together.

"I'll be right there." Then Cassie whispered, "I'm hiding my treasures." After a minute, she limped around one of the bales. "Well, what are you up to?" Cassie stopped walking when she saw Jack. "Jack, are you okay?"

He didn't answer.

"You look upset, sweetie. Is everything all right?"

Jack turned toward the door. "I'm fine. I just . . . got something in my eye when I was flying into the barn. That's all."

"You sure?"

"Yes!" Jack snapped. He took a breath in and let it back out. "I'm fine."

"Well . . . I was hoping you'd come home soon because I have something to tell you about. Mrs. Bertha, Johnny's mother, was here just a few minutes ago, and she invited us over to their nest tonight for Christmas Eve dinner! Isn't that nice?"

"I am *not* going underground, Mom."

"I thought you might say that, so I have an idea, and I want to know what you think of it. How about *I* go to the Christmas Eve dinner, and *you* go visit your dad?"

Jack immediately looked at Cassie. "I . . . I

don't want you to be alone for Christmas, Mom."

"But I won't be, dear! I'll be with Bertha and her family! And Bertha said they're inviting Mrs. Mole over too, so I won't feel out of place with their family at all! You and I can spend this afternoon together, and then you can go to your dad's when I leave for the dinner party. Sound okay? You can come back home tomorrow after breakfast, so we can be together on Christmas Day too. What do you think?"

Jack didn't speak or move. This was exactly what he wanted—what he needed. But he didn't want to seem too eager and hurt his mom. She'd think that he'd rather be in the fields with his dad and not with her. "Yeah, okay. If that's what you want," Jack answered lightly.

CHAPTER 12

Jack's Gift

Jack and Cassie ate lunch together. When they finished eating, Cassie pulled out her collection *again* and showed every trinket to Jack. As Cassie held up each item, Jack got an idea.

He thought about the metal star on top of Madelyn and Derek's Christmas tree in the yard. Jack decided that when his mom left for Bertha's

Christmas Eve dinner, he'd go and get that star. He'd leave it in their stall as a Christmas gift for his mom. Jack almost smiled thinking about how surprised and excited his mom would be when she found the star after dinner.

When the sun was low in the sky, Cassie and Jack headed out of the barn. They stopped just inside the large sliding doors. Cassie looked over at the house's driveway. It was filled with vehicles. "I wonder what the house family has going on this evening?" Cassie thought aloud.

"They have their whole big family over for Christmas Eve. They're all coming outside tonight to have a bonfire. I heard the house kids say they're all going to sing around the fire. Maybe you'll be able to hear them when you get back from Bertha's."

"That's *Mrs.* Bertha's—let's use our manners, son. Oh, I hope I do hear them singing Christmas songs! That'll be so nice! Maybe I'll go to sleep listening to the pretty music. This is going to be a wonderful Christmas, Jack! I hope you have a great time with your dad."

Cassie wrapped her good wing around Jack and gave him a long hug. "I love you so very much, Jack."

"I love you too, Mom."

Cassie slowly headed to Bertha's nest as Jack

flew toward the cornfields. He flew over the house and landed on the mailbox. Jack planned to wait there until his mom was at Bertha's.

"What are you up to, crow?" Jack heard a familiar voice say. He looked down to see Alex, who was standing with Johnny at a fence post a few feet away.

"I'm headed to the fields to spend Christmas Eve with my dad," Jack answered.

"Oh, that's awesome!" said Johnny.

"What are you waiting here for?" asked Alex.

"My mom's headed to your house, Johnny. Once she's over there, I'm going to get the shiny star off that tree and leave it in our stall as a Christmas gift for my mom."

"I'm sure she'd love it, Jack, but that's not your star to give—it belongs to the house kids," said Johnny.

"Ah, they won't care. They probably won't even notice it's gone. And my mom will enjoy that star way more than they ever will."

Johnny started to say something to try and reason more with Jack about the star, but Alex interrupted. "Well, we better get going. The sun is setting, and old Mr. Archie will soon be out hunting. I for one don't want to be *his* Christmas Eve dinner."

Alex had learned over the last four weeks that

arguing with Jack was a waste of time. Jack did what Jack wanted to do.

"Yeah, I've got to go too. My mom will be wondering where I am," added Johnny. "I'm glad you're gonna get to see your dad, Jack. Is it a long flight to him?"

"It'll take me about two hours to get there. Dad's fields are close to those mountains." Jack nodded to the mountains south of where they were standing. "The farmer who owns Dad's fields let his kids put out this ridiculous-looking scarecrow. Like those ever keep us crows away! Dad actually sleeps on top of the scarecrow's hat!" Jack laughed.

"Well, I hope you have a good flight, and Merry Christmas, Jack," said Johnny.

"Yeah, Merry Christmas," echoed Alex.

Jack nodded. "Bye, guys."

Johnny and Alex headed toward their homes, and Jack flew to the Christmas tree in the yard. As he flew over, Jack grabbed the star with his feet. He soared into the barn and back to his and Cassie's stall. Jack laid the star in front of the wall where Cassie hid her collection. Then he took off again and flew straight to his dad's fields.

Meanwhile, Johnny and Alex were running along the fence of the cow pasture. As they ran, they heard Ma Cow holler, "Boys? Boys, could you please help me?"

They turned to see Ma standing in the pasture. "Sure, Ma. What's up?" Alex answered as they scurried over to her.

"Are you okay, Ma?" Johnny asked.

"Well, I was just walkin' around, gettin' some fresh air, and I seem to have stepped on somethin' with my back hoof. It's hurtin' me. Could you boys please take a look and see what I've done?"

"Yes, ma'am. We sure will," answered Johnny.

Ma held up one of her back hooves for the boys to check.

"Ma, looks like you've got a small rock stuck in your hoof. Want us to yank it out?" asked Alex.

"Oh, I'd so appreciate it if you would!"

Alex tried to pull the stone out, but it was wedged tight. So Johnny gave it a try. As he was pulling, Johnny said, "I wish Jack was here. He could grab this rock with his beak or peck it out."

"I'm glad that naughty crow isn't here," said Ma. "He'd probably peck me on purpose! He's a bad crow."

Johnny let go of the stone, and Alex took another turn.

"Jack definitely does some things that I don't like, but I think he's more hurt than bad," said Johnny.

"Sweet Johnny. Don't you ever change," said Ma as she smiled at him.

"Ma? Could I try grabbing ahold of this thing with my teeth?" asked Alex. "I'll be real careful not to bite you."

"Yes, young'un. I trust you."

Alex got his teeth around the rock and gave it a very hard pull. Out it came! Ma set her foot back down on the ground as Alex spit out the stone.

"Oh, that feels *sooo* much better! How can I ever thank you two boys?"

"We're happy to help you, Ma! Have a Merry Christmas!" said Johnny as he and Alex started toward their homes again.

"Merry Christmas, Ma!" hollered Alex.

"Merry Christmas, boys!" Ma called back. "Sweet, sweet boys," she said softly to herself.

Around seven p.m., the house family and all their guests came out to the backyard. Jim, the house dad, lit the bonfire in the firepit. The large family all took their seats. There were seventeen adults and children around the fire.

No one minded the cold. The fire, hot chocolate, and laughter warmed everyone—inside and out. Countless s'mores were made and devoured.

After their snack, the family sang Christmas carols—one after another. No one around that bonfire was in a hurry to leave. Everything felt just so perfect. Nobody wanted it to end.

After the eleventh song, Iva Jo said, "Let's sing just one more, and then we need to call it a night. Santa will be on his way soon!"

Madelyn, Derek, and their cousins squealed and clapped their hands.

"Let's finish with singing 'Silent Night,'" said Madelyn and Derek's nana.

As the beautiful sound filled the cold night, Cassie hobbled into her stall. She'd had such a wonderful evening with Bertha's family. Cassie went to the wall to check her treasures and, to her absolute delight, found the shiny metal star that Jack had left. Cassie picked it up and hugged it. "Jack," she whispered.

CHAPTER 13

Call 9-1-1!

When the family finished singing, everyone headed inside the house except for Madelyn, Derek, and their dad. Jim handed the water-filled buckets to Madelyn and Derek. The fire had burned down quite a lot, with only glowing embers remaining.

"Madelyn, you stand on this side of the firepit,

and Derek, you go to the other side," Jim directed.

Madelyn and Derek did as they were told.

"Dad, will you count to three so we can both pour our water at the same time?" Derek asked.

"Sure," Jim answered.

Derek and Madelyn both held their buckets waist level, ready to pour.

"One . . . two . . . three," Jim counted. When he said "three," the kids poured water on the embers as smoke surrounded them.

"Good job. You can just set the buckets down here. I'll put them away later." Jim inspected the fire to make sure it was completely out. "All right, let's head on in so we can say goodbye to everyone before they leave. Make sure you thank them again for your gifts."

"Yes, sir!" Madelyn and Derek answered as they ran to the house.

As the kids hugged their family and wished them all a Merry Christmas in the house, Cassie hummed to herself in the barn as she polished her new star. Using her good wing, Cassie rubbed her feathers all over the star. She was so happy with this new addition.

Cassie decided to get her entire collection out of her hiding spot. Using her beak, Cassie pulled each item from the crack at the base of the wall. She placed them in a line on the floor.

Cassie slowly hobbled down the line, taking time to look at and enjoy each treasure. She had a dime, a silver gum wrapper, a paper clip, a brass button, a hair barrette, a balled-up piece of foil, an icicle ornament, two bottle caps, and a silver earring. But nothing in the collection was as beautiful to her as the metal star from Jack.

Cassie polished each trinket one more time before bed. She started with the dime and slowly moved her way down the line. She would polish the star last and then hide everything in the crack at the bottom of the wall.

Madelyn and Derek ran upstairs to their rooms and put on their Christmas pajamas. Once they were dressed for bed, they came down to the kitchen to help their mom with Santa's milk and cookies.

Iva Jo got Santa's plate and mug out of the

cabinet. The plate was red-and-white striped, like a candy cane, and the mug was red.

Madelyn and Derek couldn't agree on which cookie Santa would like better, so they left him two different kinds. Madelyn set a frosted sugar cookie on one side of Santa's plate while Derek put a chocolate chip cookie on the other side. They also got eight carrots from the fridge and placed those on a paper plate for Santa's reindeer.

Once the milk, cookies, and carrots were set out on the coffee table in the family room, Madelyn and Derek joined their mom and dad on the couch. Jim opened his Bible and read the Christmas story from Luke chapter two. Madelyn and Derek both snuggled up to their mom. They listened to their dad read as they watched the lights twinkle on the Christmas tree in front of them.

When Jim finished reading, he closed the Bible and said, "All right, you two, time for bed." He looked down at his watch. "I bet Santa will be here soon."

Jim smiled at his wife as Madelyn and Derek jumped off the couch and ran up to their rooms yelling, "Good night! Love you!"

"Good night, Madelyn! Good night, Derek! I love you both!" Iva Jo called to them.

Jim laid the Bible on the coffee table and stood up. He closed his eyes and stretched his back. "I'm gonna go check on the animals and shut the barn door before the rain starts," he told Iva Jo.

Jim went through the kitchen and out the back door. The screen door shut behind him. Only seconds after it shut, Jim yanked the door back open and yelled, "Iva Jo! Call 9-1-1! The barn is on fire!"

CHAPTER 14

The Barn

Sometimes in life, things happen at precisely the perfect moment. As Jim jumped off the porch and frantically ran to the barn, it started raining. The cold, hard rain quickly extinguished the fire on the outside of the barn, but the fire inside was still spreading.

The noise of Jim yelling and the back screen door slamming brought Madelyn and Derek downstairs. They watched and listened as their mom called 9-1-1. Iva Jo told the operator about the barn and gave him their house address. "Yes. Yes, that's the correct address. I have to go help my husband now," Iva Jo said before hanging up. "Kids, you *must* stay inside this house! Do you hear me?"

"Yes, ma'am," Madelyn and Derek both answered. Their eyes were huge.

Iva Jo ran out the back door. Madelyn and Derek hurried through the kitchen. They grabbed each other's hand as they stood at the door, watching their mom run through the rain to the barn.

When Iva Jo made it to the sliding doors, she saw that the fire had already consumed about half of the barn. The flames had quickly devoured the dry hay stored at the back.

Jim stood in the aisle with a hose, spraying water onto a massive wall of flames. Iva Jo ran to Ma Cow's stall and unlocked the door. The smoke was so thick that Iva Jo could barely even see the large cow. "Come on, Ma!" she yelled. Ma came out of her stall and followed Iva Jo out into the pasture.

Jim kept fighting the flames with the hose as

Iva Jo went back and forth, letting the animals out of their stalls. As Iva Jo led the last two goats through the barn's doors, she heard Jim yell, "It's out! I think the fire's out now!"

Iva Jo led the goats to the pasture as Jim came out of the barn. He turned and stared at what remained. After closing the gate, Iva Jo went to stand next to him in the rain.

As Madelyn and Derek watched their parents through the back door's window, Derek asked, "Is it over?"

"I think so."

Madelyn and Derek heard the faint sound of a siren. It was growing louder every second.

"That must be the fire truck," said Madelyn.

About ten seconds later, a large red fire truck pulled into their driveway. Maurice, the fire chief, jumped down from the truck and ran through the rain to Jim and Iva Jo.

"Jim!" Maurice shouted. "Is the fire out?"

"I believe so! Thank God for this rain!" Jim yelled back.

Maurice motioned to his crew. "We'll make sure!"

Madelyn and Derek watched from the back door as the firefighters went toward the barn.

"Derek," Madelyn said. She nervously swallowed. "Was this *our* fault?"

The firefighters confirmed that the fire was completely out. They couldn't tell what had started it yet, but there seemed to be no signs of foul play.

Jim, Iva Jo, and Maurice stepped out of the rain and onto the house's back porch.

"Maurice, thanks for coming so quickly," Jim said.

Maurice nodded. "I'm sure sorry about your barn, but I'm thankful all the animals are safe. We'll go through everything and figure out what caused the fire."

"Maurice, it's cold and wet," said Iva Jo. "Why don't y'all just come back once the rain has stopped? There's nothing more that can be done at this point. And it's Christmas Eve. Y'all go on home and spend Christmas with your families."

"That's mighty kind of you. Right when this rain lets up, we'll come back to investigate more. Weather forecast is showing it should stop around nine a.m."

"I'm so sorry we're taking y'all away from your families at Christmas," said Iva Jo.

"Ma'am, we signed up for this. It's just a part of the job. We'll see you folks in the morning when the rain stops."

The house family didn't sleep much that Christmas Eve night. Jim called the Haynie family, their neighbors, and asked if the animals could stay in the Haynies' barn for the time being. Jim was relieved but not surprised when Bo Haynie told him that they could.

Jim started loading the animals into his cattle trailer. As he was loading Ma Cow, Bo showed up with his trailer to help. Between the two trailers, Jim and Bo were able to get all of the animals over to the Haynies' barn in one trip.

Jim returned home around one a.m. Iva Jo and the kids were waiting up for him. They all felt too flustered to sleep, but about an hour later, sleep finally came.

CHAPTER 15

Mrs. Cassie

Crows typically wake with the sunrise. Jack opened his eyes and looked out over the cold, barren cornfield. Jack had slept on the shoulder of the scarecrow. His father had slept in his usual spot—on top of the scarecrow's head. Jack looked back and saw his dad waking up.

"Dad, after breakfast, I'm gonna head back to see Mom."

"You sure you don't want to stay longer? It's been fun having you here, son."

Jack smiled but quickly looked away from his dad. "I wish I could, but Mom will get all out of sorts if I don't get back soon."

"Yeah, I know how she can be . . ."

The sun had also just come up at the house, revealing the full damage of the barn. The rain was still falling, but not nearly as hard as it had been.

The yard animals knew about the fire. They had watched helplessly as the barn burned. They also saw Jim and Bo load up the barn animals.

Johnny and Alex met under the big tree near the fence. The tree gave them a little shelter from the rain.

"I don't know if saying Merry Christmas is appropriate or not after what's happened," said Johnny.

"That was awful," Alex said as he stared at what remained of the barn. "I counted the

91

animals as the house dad loaded them, and I think all of the barn animals are okay."

"But what about Mrs. Cassie?" Johnny asked.

"I know, I thought of her too. I hope she got out of the barn somehow."

"When we smelled the smoke last night, we looked out of our nest to see what was happening. We saw that the fire had already burned through Mrs. Cassie and Jack's end of the barn." Johnny looked down at his feet before continuing. "Mom asked my dad to go check on Mrs. Cassie last night while the house dad was loading up the animals."

"Did he go? With Mr. Archie being awake?" Alex asked.

"Yeah, he went. He promised Mom that he'd be really careful."

"Your dad's brave," Alex said in awe.

"He is." Johnny looked over at the barn. "He didn't find Mrs. Cassie anywhere."

Alex was quiet for a moment before saying, "But with all that rain and smoke, it may have been hard for him to see where she was hiding."

Alex and Johnny stood in silence for a minute.

"You wanna go check?" Johnny asked.

Alex shifted on his feet. "What if we find . . . something?"

"I know, I'm worried about that too. But you know Jack will be here soon. I'd like to be able to tell him that . . . we tried."

Alex took a deep breath and let it out. "Yeah, let's go."

Johnny and Alex hurried through the wet grass. They stopped at the sliding doors. The barn was much brighter inside than usual because the entire back wall was no longer there.

"Let's go," said Johnny. Just as he and Alex stepped through the doors, they heard a woosh of wings. They turned to see Jack landing behind them. His face showed confused horror.

"Wha . . . what happened?" Jack said in a whisper.

Johnny hopped toward him. "Jack, there was a fire last night—"

"Where's my mom? Where's Mom?" Jack interrupted.

Johnny looked over at Alex and then back to Jack. "Jack, no one has been able to find her yet."

Jack immediately took off flying to the rubble that used to be his and Cassie's stall. "Mom! Mom!" Jack cawed as he flew.

Johnny and Alex scurried after him. They checked under fallen, charred wood while calling out, "Mrs. Cassie? Mrs. Cassie?"

The three boys searched every foot of the barn. Then Jack flew out into the rain. He called for his mom all around the yard. Johnny and Alex watched helplessly from the opening of the barn doors.

"This is horrible," Alex whispered to Johnny.

Johnny nodded as a tear fell from his eye.

After a few minutes, Jack landed in front of Johnny and Alex. Jack breathed heavily as he stared at the ground.

"Jack . . . Jack, I'm so sorry," said Johnny.

"Me too," whispered Alex.

Jack looked up at Johnny. Jack's eyes were filled with tears, but his face was filled with rage. "How did the fire start?" Jack asked in an emotionless voice.

"I . . . I don't know," Johnny answered.

Jack looked over at the house. "It was those kids. Their bonfire. They . . . they didn't put it out. Those kids killed my mom." Jack looked back at Johnny. "Those kids killed my mom!"

Tears fell from Jack's eyes. Without another word, he took off flying toward the cornfields.

CHAPTER 16

Who Started the Fire?

The rain stopped completely just after nine a.m. True to his word, Chief Maurice and a couple of the firefighters returned to the barn shortly after. Jim met them outside.

"Mornin', Jim. I see you moved all the animals," said Maurice.

"Yeah, Bo Haynie and I moved them all last

night over to his barn."

"That's good. Well, we'll get started and try to figure out what caused the fire," Maurice said as he and the firefighters headed toward the barn.

"Can I help y'all with anything?" Jim asked.

"No, we've got it. I'll let you know if we find something. You go on in and enjoy this Christmas morning with those two kids of yours."

"It's not been a very enjoyable morning so far. Madelyn and Derek are both pretty torn up. There's been a lot tears. They're afraid *they* started the fire. See, we had a bonfire last night," said Jim. "They poured water on the fire to put it out before we all came in. I checked it, Maurice. The fire was completely out."

"Where is your firepit?"

Jim pointed over past the barn.

"We'll start over there and see if the fire made a trail over to the barn," said Maurice. "I can tell from here that your firepit is a safe distance from your barn, so a floating ember couldn't have traveled that far."

Maurice and the firefighters headed over to the firepit as Jim went back in the house. Johnny and Alex had been listening and watching from the fence in the backyard.

"Do you think the house kids' bonfire did this?" Alex asked Johnny.

"I sure hope not."

About five minutes later, they watched Chief Maurice leave the firepit area and head to the house's back porch. Maurice knocked on the door. Jim and Iva Jo both answered.

"Could y'all get Madelyn and Derek, please? I'm pretty sure they're gonna wanna hear this," Maurice said.

Johnny and Alex wanted to hear it too. They scurried over to the picnic table so they could hear better.

Madelyn and Derek joined their parents on the back porch with Chief Maurice.

"Kids, your dad told me that you're worried about what started the barn fire."

"Yes, sir," Madelyn answered with tear-filled eyes. Derek nodded in agreement.

Both kids held their breath as Chief Maurice said, "Well, we've checked around the firepit, and I want to tell you both that your bonfire did *not* catch the barn on fire."

Madelyn and Derek both breathed out heavily. Jim patted Derek on the back as Iva Jo hugged Madelyn.

"Thank you, Maurice," said Jim. "But then, what do you think caused the fire? There wasn't any lightning here last night."

"We haven't gone through the barn yet. I

wanted to go ahead and let these two know," Maurice said as he looked at Madelyn and Derek, "that they didn't do anything wrong. We'll start going through the barn now and see what we can find."

"Thank you, Chief Maurice," said Madelyn.

"Yeah, thank you!" echoed Derek.

"Excuse me, sir?" someone called.

Maurice turned to see one of the firefighters standing at the steps of the porch. She had something in her hands. Maurice went down the steps to talk to her.

"What's going on, Dad?" Derek whispered.

"I'm not sure. Maybe they've already found something," Jim answered.

After a minute, Maurice said, "Folks, this is Lieutenant Berry. She has something to show y'all that will explain how that fire started."

Lieutenant Berry held up a piece of electrical wire with a metal star sticking out of it. "It appears you had a bird in your barn who liked to collect shiny objects," she said. Lieutenant Berry opened her other hand to reveal a dime, a paper clip, a brass button, a hair barrette, a balled-up piece of foil, two bottle caps, and a silver earring. "We found all of this where the back barn wall used to be. It appears that the bird hid its collection there. When it tried to hide this star, it stabbed an electrical wire."

"That star is from the tree we decorated in the yard!" said Derek.

Iva Jo looked over at Jim and whispered, "My hurt crow?"

Jim nodded back to her.

Iva Jo looked down, closed her eyes, and shook her head.

"Chief Maurice, what happened when the bird did that? Is the bird okay?" Madelyn asked.

"No, I'm afraid the bird would have died instantly," Maurice answered.

"That poor bird," said Madelyn softly.

"But at least if the bird died instantly, I'm sure it didn't feel any pain at all," Iva Jo said as she patted Madelyn's back.

As the people continued talking on the porch, Alex turned to Johnny. "So . . . Mrs. Cassie killed herself?" Alex asked in a shocked whisper.

"Yes, but she didn't mean to, of course," Johnny answered.

Alex looked at the ground in disbelief. "How awful." He quickly looked up at Johnny. "We have to let Jack know! The kids *didn't* do it!" Alex's excitement suddenly lessened. "Oh, but how do we tell Jack that his mom was the one who started the fire that killed her?"

"Yep. And how do we tell him that she started the fire with the gift *he* left for her?" Johnny added.

Both stood in silence as they watched the people on the back porch.

"Well," Johnny eventually said. He took a big breath and let it out. "We just have to tell him. Jack has to know." Johnny looked at Alex. "We'll do it together. We'll tell Jack first thing when he comes back."

But Jack never came back.

CHAPTER 17

The Letters

Eleven months passed. Many things changed in that time. The barn was rebuilt. The animals came back home from the Haynies' barn. Madelyn and Derek were a year older. Johnny and Alex were also a year older.

Although eleven months is the same amount of

time for people and animals, those months bring different changes. Madelyn and Derek had both moved up a grade at school. They had grown inches taller. They had lost more baby teeth. But they were still kids.

Johnny and Alex, however, were no longer children. Eleven months for some animals turns them into adults. That November found Johnny married and a father to five daughters. Alex hadn't met his squirrel yet, but he had his eyes open. One thing that had not changed, though, was that Johnny and Alex were still best friends.

It was the day after Thanksgiving. Johnny had told his girls all about Santa Claus and how the house kids would mail letters to him on the day after Thanksgiving. Johnny's daughters wanted to see Madelyn and Derek mail their Santa letters. Johnny asked Alex if he'd like to come along.

The mailman always came to the house a little after nine a.m. Johnny wasn't sure what time Madelyn and Derek would bring their letters to the mailbox, so at seven a.m., Johnny, his girls, and Alex were all waiting at the fence behind the mailbox.

"When are dey gonna come, Uncle Alwex?" Bonnie, Johnny's tiniest daughter, asked.

Alex picked Bonnie up and put her on his shoulders. "I'm sure it'll be soon. I bet they're just finishing up their breakfast now, and then they'll head on out here to mail their letters."

"What do you think they'll ask Santa for?" asked Cassie. Cassie was Johnny's oldest daughter. Johnny had named her after Mrs. Cassie.

"Maybe they'll ask him for a slide!" Johnny suggested. "Then you five could play on it when the house family isn't outside!"

Johnny's daughters hopped up and down.

Alex saw movement at the front porch. "Oh, girls, I think they're coming out!"

All seven of them hid behind the fence posts. They watched as Madelyn and Derek ran to the mailbox. Derek opened the box. He and Madelyn set their letters inside. Derek closed the mailbox as Madelyn pulled up its flag. Then she gave Derek a high five.

Johnny's daughters all giggled and wiggled as they watched Madelyn and Derek run back to their house.

"All right, my darlings, time to head home," Johnny said as Alex set Bonnie back down on the ground.

"Aww, but, Daddy, I wanna see de mailman come and get duh Santa letters," Bonnie said with a frown on her little face.

"Sweetie, that would mean we'd have to stand here for like another hour and a half. We'd get pretty bored just standing here. Besides, I need to help your uncle Alex find some pecans to take to his mother. You five go on home now. Love you, girls," Johnny said as he hugged each of them.

Johnny and Alex went with the girls as they crossed the street, but they stopped in the front yard as the girls hopped on home. Alex and Johnny made their game plan for the pecan haul.

Johnny said, "Do you want me to go grab some of the fallen magnolia leaves for us to stack the pecans on while you . . ." Johnny stopped talking. Something at the mailbox had caught his attention.

Alex had his back to the mailbox, but he turned to follow Johnny's gaze. Alex saw something black on top of the mailbox.

It was a black bird. Using its wing, the bird lowered the mailbox's flag. Then with its beak, it opened the mailbox. It leaned down and pulled Madelyn and Derek's letters out. The bird rose back up with the letters in its beak.

Johnny hopped a little closer to the mailbox. "Jack?" he called out.

Jack quickly turned his head toward Johnny and stared at him. Jack's expression slowly turned into an evil grin. With the letters in his beak, he took off flying to the cornfields.

"Johnny," Alex said as he ran to stand next to him. "Jack just stole Madelyn and Derek's Santa letters! W-why would he do that?"

"Revenge," Johnny answered solemnly. "Jack's trying to hurt them, trying to get back at them because of his mom." Johnny looked at Alex. "He still blames them for the fire. We never got a chance to tell Jack that the kids didn't do it."

"Johnny, Christmas morning is going to come, and the house kids won't have any presents from Santa. They'll think they've been bad. They'll be . . . devastated!" Alex became angry. "But *they're* not the bad ones! Jack's always been a bad crow!"

Johnny looked down. "Jack is hurt, and his hurt has turned into anger. He thinks hurting the house kids will make him feel better." Johnny looked up at Alex. "But it won't. We have to tell him what really happened to his mom. If Jack knew the truth, I know he wouldn't want to hurt the house kids."

"Oh, you *know* that? I think he'd still want to hurt them. I think he likes being mean. He likes doing mean things. Did you see that smile Jack gave you before he flew off? He's bad, Johnny. And we have to stop him." Alex looked at the house. "We have to get those letters back."

105

CHAPTER 18

You Want Me to Do What?

Johnny and Alex went to the quiet barn so they could figure out how they'd get the letters back from Jack. Alex leaned against one of the stall doors while Johnny hopped back and forth, thinking.

"We know where Jack's taken the letters. I bet

anything he's taken them back to his dad to show him and brag," Alex said as he watched Johnny.

Johnny didn't speak. He was deep in thought.

"And we know where his dad is," Alex continued. "In the cornfields close to the mountain that's about two hours from here."

Again, Johnny said nothing. He just kept hopping back and forth.

"And we know that you and I would probably never find the scarecrow where Jack's dad sleeps. It could take us hours, if not days, to search the fields for that scarecrow. And that would mean we'd be out in the fields at night. I, for one, do not want to see an owl."

Johnny stopped hopping and stared at Alex.

"What?" Alex asked.

Johnny didn't answer, but his nose started twitching.

"Johnny, what? Your nose tells me you've thought of something."

"I have, but you're not gonna like it," Johnny answered.

Alex leaned forward.

"We need an owl," said Johnny.

"I'm sorry, what? I think I just went crazy. I could have sworn you said we needed an *owl*."

"That's exactly what he said, sugar." Ma Cow

raised her head over her stall door and said, "And I think I know why. I also think I know the perfect owl to help you . . . Archie."

Alex slowly stood to his feet. "I don't know what you two are thinking, but I can tell you right now that if the plan to get those letters back involves an owl . . . I'm out. Count me out!"

Johnny hopped over to Alex. "Alex, you're right. You and I'd probably never be able to find that scarecrow. We need the help of someone who's seen all of the cornfields from above. Who probably knows where all the scarecrows are. And who can get there much quicker than you and I can alone. Alex, we need Mr. Archie's help."

"And who's gonna ask him? You? It definitely won't be me! And you probably wouldn't even get a chance to ask him. He'd probably *eat* you before you got the question out of your mouth!"

"Boys, *I'll* ask him," Ma interjected.

Johnny and Alex both looked up at Ma.

"Archie owes me a favor. He'll help you two if I ask him."

"He owes you a favor?" Alex asked. He and Johnny glanced at each other. Alex looked back up at Ma and asked, "What does he owe you a favor for?"

"I saved his life when he was younger. He's never forgotten it. He's always told me that if I ever need anythang to just let him know, and I could consider it done."

Johnny asked, "How did you save his life?"

"Oh, sugar, that is a very long story. One that I'll tell you both another time. Now, what do I need to ask Archie to do?"

"You need to ask him to not eat us, for one thing!" Alex said emphatically.

"Ma, please ask Mr. Archie if he can take us to the scarecrow in the fields near the mountain. I'm sure there's more than one, but who knows, maybe Mr. Archie has seen Jack, his dad, and their crow . . . friends sleeping on one of the scarecrows. That's where we have to go. Jack has stolen the house kids' Santa letters, and we have to get them back."

Ma frowned. "That Jack always was a bad crow. I sure did like Mrs. Cassie, though, and I miss her somethin' awful. But I do *not* miss that Jack. I'll tell Archie all about this right when he wakes up at sundown. You boys come back here after the sun has set, and I guarantee you, Archie will be here waitin' to help you."

Ma looked down at Alex. "Alex, owls are very noble, honest birds. If Archie gives me his word that he won't hurt you, he won't hurt you at all. I promise, darlin'."

Johnny and Alex left the barn to gather the

109

pecans for Alex's mom. They delivered the nuts and then headed back to their homes. They agreed to meet at the fence in front of the barn just before sunset.

As the sun was just about to pass below the tree line, Alex and Johnny met at the fence.

"I can't believe we're doing this, Johnny."

"Like you said, we have to get the house kids' letters back, and this is the only way to make that happen," said Johnny. "I've had more time to think all of this through, and I think I've got a solid plan now."

"Does your plan still involve Mr. Archie? Please say no."

Johnny grinned at his friend. "It does." Johnny put his paw on Alex's back. "And you'll be fine."

"Wait." Alex moved away from Johnny. "*You'll* be fine? Don't you mean, *we'll* be fine?"

Johnny took a breath. "Like I said, I've had time to think all of this through, and I need you to go with Mr. Archie tonight . . . without me."

"You want me to do what?"

CHAPTER 19

Two Reasons

Johnny hopped toward Alex. "I can't go with you and Mr. Archie tonight."

"Why not?" Alex asked.

"I . . . I'll be busy doing something else." Johnny shuffled his feet.

"What?"

"I can't tell you right now," Johnny answered.

"You *can't* tell me, or you *won't* tell me?"

Johnny let out an exasperated sigh. "Okay, I won't tell you."

"Why?"

"For a couple of reasons, Alex. For one thing, the sun is almost completely gone, and Mr. Archie will be waiting on us. We need to get going," Johnny said as he started hopping toward the barn.

Alex jumped in front of Johnny, blocking his way. "You said a couple reasons. What's the second reason?"

Johnny looked down for a moment and then back up at Alex. "The other reason is that if I tell you what I need to do, I'm afraid you're going to talk me out of doing it. It's . . . well, what I have to do is very dangerous. Probably a lot more dangerous than you being with Mr. Archie. But it's the only way to get the house kids' letters back and stop Jack."

Alex didn't know what to say to that. This letter-rescue mission was turning into something way more dangerous than he ever thought it would be. Alex liked the house kids. He genuinely did, but was the house kids' happiness worth him and Johnny risking their lives?

As if Johnny were reading Alex's mind,

Johnny said, "You know, I was thinking this afternoon that maybe we shouldn't try to get the house kids' letters back. I mean, I want them to get their gifts from Santa, and I don't want them to be sad. But is all of that worth risking our lives for?"

Johnny looked at the house. "But then I got to thinking, this is more than just getting their letters back. You and I both know that when we get those letters from Jack, he'll come back after them again. He's not one to take losing lying down. And we *need* Jack to come back so we can tell him what really happened to his mom. He has to know, Alex. Because if he doesn't learn the truth about what happened . . ." Johnny stopped.

"What? What were you going to say?" asked Alex.

"I don't think Jack would ever try to physically hurt the kids. I hope his revenge games stop with just taking their Santa letters. But . . . but what if I'm wrong? It's been almost a year since Mrs. Cassie's accident. She was the only constant positive influence in Jack's life. Who knows where Jack's thoughts have taken him this past year? We just . . . we have to stop him. I hope telling Jack what really happened to his mom will do that."

Johnny put his paw on Alex's shoulder. "Come on," Johnny said calmly. "Let's go talk with Mr. Archie."

Alex and Johnny slowly made their way to the barn. They'd never been there at night. Like all small critters, Johnny and Alex usually stayed in their nests after sundown. Nighttime belonged to owls, coyotes, racoons, and possums.

As Johnny and Alex made their way through the large barn doors, they saw the terrifying but majestic vision of Archie sitting on top of Ma Cow's stall door. This sight made Johnny's and Alex's already fast-beating hearts start to race.

Archie was an extremely large barn owl. He had a pronounced beak, darker than most barn owls' beaks. His eyes were black and round. He had a white face. His wings were a mix of gray and tan feathers. But to Johnny and Alex, Archie's most mesmerizing feature was his extremely large sharp talons.

Johnny hopped over to Ma Cow's stall and bravely looked up at the owl.

"Hello, Mr. Archie. I know we've never met before . . ."

"Thankfully," Alex muttered.

". . . but I've known of you my entire life. My name is Johnny, and this"—Johnny nodded over at Alex—"is my good friend, Alex."

114

Alex moved a couple of inches closer.

Archie stared down at Johnny. He slowly spread his massive wings and jumped from the stall door. He landed in between Johnny and Alex. Ma Cow raised her head over her door and looked down at the three.

Facing Johnny, Archie said, "I can't say that I've ever met a rabbit and a squirrel in this type of setting before, but I'm glad to meet you both. Ma has explained the situation to me, and I've given her my word that I will not hurt either of you."

Archie turned to face Alex. Alex took a large step backward.

"Alex, are you okay?" Ma asked.

Alex swallowed. "I feel like I keep breathing in, but I'm unable to breathe out." Alex looked up at Archie. "You are truly terrifying, sir."

Archie smiled and let out a little chuckle. "I promise you, Alex, I'll bring you home safely tonight." Archie looked back at Ma Cow. "I gave Ma my word. I've been looking for a way to repay her for years. I'm very thankful that she's finally made a request of me."

Ma nodded her approval at Archie. She looked at Alex and comfortingly said, "Alex, you'll be just fine, sugar."

Archie turned back to Johnny. "There are two

scarecrows in the cornfields close to the mountain," said Archie. "I've seen them a few times when hunting around there."

Alex's tummy did a flip-flop at that statement.

"One of those scarecrows has to be where Jack sleeps. I'm assuming we're going to sneak up and take the letters back, correct?" Archie asked.

"Yes, sir. But I won't be going with you and Alex. I have to stay behind and get another part of our plan set up. So it'll just be you and Alex," Johnny answered.

Archie looked back at Alex. "*Yaaaay*," Alex said softly.

Archie smiled. "Well, if we're wanting Jack and any other crows there to be in a deep sleep when we come, we may want to wait a couple of hours before we leave. That okay with you, Alex?" Archie asked.

"Yes, I'm okay with that."

"All right, then. I'm going out to hunt," Archie said. "I'll hopefully eat a quick meal before we set off. I'll be back soon." Archie spread his huge wings and took off over Alex's head.

Alex stared wide-eyed at Johnny.

Johnny's nose twitched as he said, "Well, at least Mr. Archie won't be hungry when you're with him."

Alex scowled. "You are not funny."

116

CHAPTER 20

Johnny's Important Question

Johnny and Alex sat on the barn floor, leaning back on Ma's door as they waited for Archie to return. Ma had stayed up with the boys to keep them company for over an hour, but she'd drifted off to sleep a little while ago. The night was quiet, and the cool air was still.

"Johnny," Alex said softly. "What is the dangerous thing you have to do while I'm gone?"

Johnny was staring out the barn doors at the house. "I guess I do need to tell you because I have to ask you a very important question." Johnny looked back at Alex. "Alex, if things don't go well for me tonight, will you please help take care of my wife and girls?"

"Good grief, Johnny!" Alex exclaimed.

"Shhh," Johnny said as he motioned his head up toward Ma Cow's door opening.

Alex regained control of his voice and whispered, "Johnny, whatever you're thinking of doing, if it's *that* dangerous, don't do it!"

"Answer me, Alex. Will you take care of my wife and girls?"

Alex stared wide-eyed at his best friend. "You know I will, but what on earth are you going to do while I'm gone? Can I . . . can I swap missions with you?"

Johnny smiled at his friend. "No, but thank you. You have to go get the letters. If they're up high on the scarecrow or something like that, I won't be able to get to them. I can't climb." Johnny looked again at the house. "Like I said earlier, you know that Jack will come for those letters once he finds they're gone. When he does, how could we stop him from just taking them out of the mailbox again?"

"I . . . I don't know. We'd have to fight him, I guess."

"I've thought of a way to ensure that tomorrow morning, the mailman gets those letters," said Johnny confidently.

"How?" Alex asked.

Johnny turned back to Alex and said, "We need Bridgett's help."

"What?" Alex shouted and sprang to his feet.

"What was that? Somethin' wrong?" Ma sleepily asked as she raised her head over her door. "You boys okay down there?"

"Oh, we're fine, Ma. I'm sorry. We just . . . just thought we saw something, but it was only a shadow." Johnny smiled up at Ma. "We're a bit jumpy tonight, that's all."

"My sweet boys, you both have nothin' to worry about. Archie will keep Alex safe. I just know he will."

"Yes, ma'am. I'm sorry we woke you. You go right on back to sleep, and we'll see you in the morning," Johnny replied.

"Night, boys," Ma said, and then she pulled her head back over her door.

Johnny motioned for Alex to follow him away from Ma's door, closer to the barn's entrance.

"Archie *and* Bridgett? The Beast?" Alex

whispered harshly. "You really are trying to get us both killed!"

"I am not. But it's actually Archie, Bridgett, and Honey."

Alex threw his paws out to his sides in confused exasperation. "I don't know what kind of plan you've concocted, but let me just say, it's a very *bad* plan!"

"No, Alex, it's not. It's the only way to make all of this work. The only way to keep Jack from taking those letters again is if we have a certain animal guarding them. That's where Bridgett comes in. We're going to put the letters back into the mailbox and have Bridgett sit on the mailbox to guard them."

"And just how are you going to get that beast cat to sit on the mailbox? She will eat you, Johnny, before you even get a chance to ask her to do it!"

"That's where Honey comes into the plan. The house family has to let Honey out to go to the bathroom before bed tonight. When they do, I'm going to ask Honey to help us—that's why I keep looking over at the house. I can't miss them letting her out in the backyard.

Honey's too old to chase me, and I've never heard of her eating any of the yard animals before, even when she was young. So I think I'll be safe talking to her. I'm going to explain the situation and ask Honey to get Bridgett to help us."

"Johnny, you may get Honey to help, but do you really think Honey can get that evil monster to help us? *And* not eat us?"

Johnny looked over at the house. "It's obvious that Bridgett loves the house kids. I think she'll do it to help protect *them*. As far as her not eating us . . . I'm just gonna hope Honey will help us with that."

As Johnny finished his sentence, Archie flew into the barn and landed next to them. "Are you ready, Alex?" Archie asked.

Alex looked at Johnny. "Yeah, I'm ready." Alex cautiously climbed up on Archie's back and hung on. He looked down at his friend. "Johnny . . ."

"You be careful, and remember what you promised me," said Johnny.

Alex closed his eyes for a moment and took a deep breath. He looked again at Johnny. "You be careful too, and I *will* see you when we get back."

With that, Alex gripped Archie's feathers. Archie spread his wings and took off into the night. There was a full moon and not a cloud in the sky.

Alex had "flown" through the trees before, but he'd never experienced anything like this. The moon and stars were so bright that Alex could see everything down below them. The trees, road, houses . . . all of it looked so small. The wind was blowing in his face.

Alex jumped when Archie suddenly said, "It's amazing up here, isn't it?"

"It really is. I've . . . I've never seen anything like this before in my life." Alex looked up. He felt so close to the moon and stars.

"There's no freedom in the world like flying," Archie said as they sailed through the air. "I always hurt for Mrs. Cassie. A bird who can't fly . . . I don't think there could be a misery in the world worse than that."

They flew in silence for a while until Archie said, "We'll fly over the closest scarecrow first. It's a good thing there aren't any clouds and that we have a full moon. We should be able to see if the crows are sleeping there without having to get very low. If they're not, we'll go check the other scarecrow."

"Okay," said Alex.

"When we find them, I'll land in the field a safe distance away, so hopefully we won't wake them. What's your plan once we land?" Archie asked.

"I'll sneak up closer to the scarecrow and hopefully see where Jack has the letters. I hope he hasn't destroyed them. If I do find the letters, I'll move as quietly as I can and try to get them.

Then I'll bring them to you, and we can head back home."

Archie nodded. "Alex, I just want to say, I admire your bravery."

"What?" Alex was surprised by that statement. He was feeling anything but brave.

"You trusting an owl and sneaking into a crow roost—all to help the house kids—that's very brave, Alex. Very brave."

Alex sat up a little taller. "Thank you, Archie."

CHAPTER 21

Alex and the Letters

Meanwhile, Johnny sat under the picnic table in the backyard, waiting for Honey to come outside. Johnny had rehearsed over and over what he planned to say to the golden retriever.

Suddenly, the screen door opened, and Honey came out onto the back porch. Johnny watched as Honey stretched before she slowly came down the steps and into the yard.

Honey sniffed around in the grass just to the left of Johnny and the picnic table. Honey lifted her head and said, "Who's there?" She sniffed again, this time moving closer to the picnic table. Honey's body moved stiffly, but there was nothing wrong with her nose.

Johnny cautiously moved out from under the table. "Mrs. Honey, my name is Johnny."

"A rabbit? You're lucky that I'm not as spry as I used to be. I don't have it in me to chase you like I would've years ago. What do you want, Johnny?"

"The house kids are in trouble."

Honey charged at Johnny and showed her teeth. When Honey was right at his face, she said, "Are you threatening my kids?"

Johnny backed up. "No, no! I'm here to *help* the kids." Johnny quickly explained what Jack had done and how he'd stolen Madelyn and Derek's Santa letters.

"What a bad crow. This squirrel who's gone to get their letters back, does he need any help?"

"Yes, ma'am. We need your help. Yours and . . . and Bri . . . Bridgett's."

"Bridgett's? You want Bridgett's help?" Honey sat down as she said, "Now, I'll help you however I can, but I don't think that high-and-mighty cat has ever helped any animal or person in her life."

125

Johnny explained how they needed Bridgett to guard the letters from Jack. "Do you think she'd help us if she knows it's for the house kids?"

Honey thought for a moment. "She may. I'll see what I can do. I could threaten to bite her if she won't help us, but she's honestly too fast for me to catch nowadays. Maybe she'll help if I tell her I'll give her all my table scraps during Christmas. We get some really good ones after those meals!"

"Yes, please try anything you can think of to get Bridgett to help us. But, Mrs. Honey, make it clear that your deal with her includes her not hurting me or my friend in any way."

"I will. I'll make that clear to her, Johnny. When do you need us back out here?"

"Honey!" Iva Jo called from the back door.

Johnny quickly whispered, "Be watching for me out the back windows when the sun comes up. Scratch at the back door when you see me motioning to you so the house family will let you outside. And be sure Bridgett comes out with you."

Honey nodded as she slowly walked back to the porch.

Alex and Archie flew over the first scarecrow. They both looked down—no crows anywhere in sight. "Must be the other one," Archie said as he turned slightly to the left.

A minute later, Archie and Alex flew over the second scarecrow. They could clearly see crows perched on the scarecrow's head and arms. There was a large tree about thirty feet away from the scarecrow. The rest of the roost was sleeping on the leafless tree.

Archie circled around the tree and landed in the field on the opposite side of the scarecrow. Alex climbed down and looked at Archie. Archie nodded at him. Alex took a deep breath and nodded back.

Alex quietly scurried through the field, toward the scarecrow. The wind had started blowing, and that helped muffle any sound Alex's feet made on the dry cornstalk remnants.

Alex paused as he studied the scarecrow. He saw a crow sleeping on top of the scarecrow's head—that had to be Jack's dad. Three crows were perched on the scarecrow's left arm, but only one crow was sleeping alone on the right arm. That lone crow was Jack.

Something white caught Alex's eye. The scarecrow had on a plaid button-up shirt. Sticking out of the shirt's chest pocket were the ends of two

127

white envelopes. Alex had found the letters!

He silently moved toward the scarecrow. When Alex reached it, he quietly climbed up the inside of one pant leg. He climbed all the way up to the neck opening of the scarecrow's shirt. Alex stuck his head out and looked over at Jack. Jack was still asleep. Alex turned to look at the other three crows. They were also still sleeping.

Alex slowly climbed out of the shirt's collar and reached down to the envelopes. He grasped both and carefully pulled them up to his mouth. Alex bit down on the envelopes and held them with his teeth, so he could use his paws to climb back down.

Before starting his descent, Alex looked back over at the three sleeping crows. None of them had moved. He then turned his head to check on Jack.

Jack was glaring at Alex. Jack cawed loudly, awakening all the crows. His caw was cut short, though, when Archie swooped in and grabbed Alex.

Archie flew as fast as he could with Alex dangling from his talons. Alex still had the envelopes sticking out of his mouth.

"Are you okay, Alex? Is how I'm holding you hurting you? Don't talk! You'll drop the letters! If you're okay, tap my foot with your paw one time."

Alex tapped Archie's foot one time.

"I'd land and let you climb up on my back, but I don't think we should stop. I'm sure Jack and his crows are out of sorts right now and forming a plan. Soon they'll set off after us. I'll get you back home as fast as I can."

Alex nodded in agreement. With his part of the plan almost complete, he could only think about Johnny. Alex hoped his friend would be there to greet him when they returned.

CHAPTER 22

Take Your Places

Alex and Archie arrived back at the barn just as the sky began to lighten. As they flew through the barn doors, Alex was relieved to see Johnny leaning against Ma's stall door. Johnny jumped to his feet the moment he saw Alex and Archie.

Archie gently set Alex down on the barn floor

and then flew to Ma's door to perch and rest from the long flight. Alex was finally able to use his arms and take the envelopes from his mouth.

Johnny hopped over to Alex and said, "You did it!" Johnny's nose twitched with joy and relief.

Alex stretched his jaw by opening and closing his mouth a couple of times. "Yep, and let me tell you, my mouth is sore. That was a long time to hold these," Alex said as he showed Johnny the two letters.

"Did you have any trouble getting them? Did Jack see you?" Johnny asked.

"He did see me. Jack woke up right when I got the letters, but Archie here"—Alex looked up at the owl—"saved me. Guess I owe you a favor now, my friend."

Archie smiled down at Alex. "If I ever need help, I know who to ask." Archie looked out the barn doors. "The sun is about to rise, so I'm going up to the rafters to sleep. Good luck, you two." Archie spread his wings and took off.

"Thank you!" Johnny and Alex called to him.

Alex turned to Johnny. "Did you get to talk to Honey? Is she in?"

"She's in."

"And what about . . . the Beast?"

"I don't know yet," Johnny answered. "Honey said last night that she'd talk to Bridgett and try to make her help us *and* not eat us. But I won't know what Bridgett decided until Honey comes outside this morning. If Honey comes out of the house alone, we'll know that Bridgett isn't going to help us."

"If Bridgett won't protect the mailbox, what will we do?" asked Alex.

"Hopefully between Honey, you, and me, we'll be able to keep Jack away from the letters until the mailman comes."

Alex's shoulders dropped. "The mailman won't come for like three more hours, Johnny." Alex looked up to where Archie had flown. "I wish Archie was still here to help us. You should have seen Jack's face when Archie swooped in and grabbed me! Jack's scared of Archie."

"Who wouldn't be?" said Johnny. He glanced out the barn doors. "The sun's coming up." He looked back at Alex. "You ready?"

Alex lightly bit down on the envelopes and held them with his teeth. He nodded.

Johnny and Alex scurried to the picnic table. Alex waited under the table as Johnny hopped out in front of it. Johnny faced the house and started waving his paws back and forth. He hoped that Honey and no one else was looking. After a few seconds, Johnny heard scratching at the kitchen door.

Johnny quickly hopped back under the table. "Honey saw me. I heard her scratching the back door so that the house family will let her out. Now we'll see if Bridgett's in on the plan or not."

Johnny and Alex stared at the back door and held their breath. Slowly, the door opened. Only Honey came out onto the porch. Johnny let out a sigh. But then they heard the house mom's voice.

"What? *You* want to go outside too? It's a bit cold. Are you sure? Okay, then," said Iva Jo.

Johnny and Alex watched as Bridgett slowly stepped out the door.

Alex took the envelopes from his mouth and whispered, "I was half hoping she wouldn't show up."

Honey quickly ran to the picnic table. Johnny and Alex came out from underneath to meet her. Bridgett sauntered down the porch steps and leisurely walked over to join them.

"Mrs. Honey, I'm so glad you saw my signal. We got the letters," Johnny said as he motioned over to Alex, who had the envelopes in his paws. "This is Alex."

"Alex, nice to meet you," said Honey. "I'm impressed that you got the children's letters back from that bird. Thanks for taking care of our kids."

Alex smiled and nodded.

He was about to speak when the Beast slowly said, "Well, well, well. If it isn't a chunky bunny and a delicious-looking squirrel at my table."

"Bridgett, stop that. You know what we talked about," Honey cautioned.

"This all was easier to agree to when I was in the house. It's much harder now that I've seen these two yummy morsels." Bridgett crouched down like she was about to pounce.

Honey barked loudly and jumped in front of Bridgett. "I may be old, but I promise you, my bite still hurts," Honey warned as she showed Bridgett her teeth.

Bridgett slowly sat back up and started grooming her paw. "Oh, hush, old lady. I just like playing with my food. I'd rather have your portion of the Christmas turkey, like you promised." Bridgett looked over at Alex. "I won't eat these two . . . today." She grinned.

"Johnny, what do we need to do?" Honey asked.

"Let's take the letters over to the mailbox, and then I'll explain everything over there," Johnny answered.

"Sounds good," Honey said as she started walking toward the front yard. Bridgett, Alex, and Johnny didn't move.

"After you," Johnny said to Bridgett.

"No, no. You two go first. I insist," said Bridgett.

"We're not letting you walk behind us—not in a million years," stated Alex.

Bridgett started to say something back, but Honey barked, "Bridgett!"

Bridgett stood and casually walked toward the front yard. Johnny and Alex followed at a good distance behind her.

At the mailbox, Johnny explained the plan. "Mrs. Honey, can Alex climb up on your back, please?"

Honey nodded and lay down on the grass. Alex put the letters into his mouth and climbed up onto her back. Honey stood up as Alex held on.

"Alex, can you reach the mailbox door to open it?" Johnny asked.

"You can climb onto my head if you need to," Honey told Alex.

Alex did as Honey offered. Honey walked over to the mailbox, and Alex opened its door.

"Good! Now just put the letters inside, close the door, and then we need to get that flag up," Johnny instructed.

Alex took the letters from his mouth, slid them into the mailbox, and closed the door. Then he jumped from Honey's head onto the top of the mailbox. Alex pulled the flag up and smiled down

135

at Johnny. Alex jumped from the mailbox back down to the ground.

"Perfect! Now, Bridgett, if you'll please sit on top of the mailbox to protect the letters," Johnny said.

Bridgett jumped onto the mailbox and lay down. "This is gonna be boring," she muttered.

"I hope it is. I hope things stay just like this for the next three hours, but they may not," said Johnny. "I don't think Jack would try to take the letters with Bridgett there, but if he brings all the crows with him . . . we may have some trouble."

"If that happens, can I at least eat the birds?" Bridgett asked.

"You absolutely can," said Alex.

"Whatever happens, don't leave the mailbox," Johnny told Bridgett. "Jack might try to use other crows to lure you away so that he can take the letters again. You can't leave your spot until those letters are safely in the mailman's hands."

Honey sat down on the back side of the mailbox to watch the field behind them. Alex sat on the right side and watched the road and sky that way. Johnny took his place on the opposite side of Alex and watched that direction. Princess Bridgett sat high up on her throne, facing the house.

136

When they were all in their places, Johnny said, "And now, we wait."

CHAPTER 23

This Was It

Hours passed, and to Johnny's joy and Bridgett's dismay, nothing happened. Bridgett had almost dozed off when she was jarred awake by Alex yelling, "I see the mailman coming!"

Johnny and Alex scurried into the grass and hid behind the fence post. Honey took Alex's spot next to the mailbox. The mail vehicle slowly pulled up.

"Well, it looks like I'm being greeted by the welcome committee this morning!" the mailman said happily. He reached down and patted Honey. Then he tickled Bridgett under her chin. He opened the mailbox and took out Madelyn and Derek's Santa letters.

As the mailman drove away, Alex sprang out of the grass and shouted, "We did it!"

Johnny hopped up next to Alex. "I'm so relieved. It's done," said Johnny.

Bridgett stood on top of the mailbox and stretched. "Yes, yes. All of this was a boring success because of me. You're all welcome." She jumped down and landed next to Johnny and Alex. Bridgett slowly walked past them, allowing her tail to rub against Alex's face. "Hope I see you two tomorrow," Bridgett sang as she walked back to the house.

"Good job, boys," Honey said. "Again, thank you for helping our kids."

"And thank *you*, Mrs. Honey," said Johnny.

"Yeah, we couldn't have done this without you," added Alex.

Honey nodded and walked back to the house, leaving Alex and Johnny standing next to the mailbox. They stood silently for a moment, just enjoying their success.

After a minute, Alex took a deep breath and let it out. "I'm tired," he said.

"You sound like you had a long night or something," Johnny said playfully, his nose twitching.

Just then, they heard a woosh of wings behind them. They turned to see Jack landing. "Well, you two stopped the big bad Jack from ruining your precious house kids' Christmas. I mean, you did have to get the help of an owl, a dog, and a cat to do it." Jack scowled at them. "But don't you both look so proud of yourselves."

"Yeah, we sure *are* proud. The house kids are going to get what they deserve—presents from Santa," said Alex, glaring back at him.

Johnny took a small hop toward Jack. "They're good kids, Jack. They really are. They—"

"Good kids?" Jack yelled. "They killed my mom, Johnny!"

"No, Jack, no! They didn't do it," Johnny started explaining. "We heard the firefighter tell the house dad what happened that awful night, and it wasn't the kids' bonfire that started the fire. Jack, it was—"

"I don't want to hear it! You two would say anything to protect your precious house kids!

You just *love* them so much!" Jack was enraged. "Well, you know who I loved? My mom! And *they* killed her!"

Johnny looked into Jack's pain-filled eyes. "You're wrong, Jack. They didn't kill her—"

Jack cawed loudly to stop Johnny from saying anything else.

Jack hopped closer to Johnny and Alex. "You two may have won this time, but I promise you, I *will* be back. I'll plan, and I'll come up with a way to ruin their Christmas next year."

Johnny lowered his head and stared at the ground.

Jack glanced over at the house. "Who knows, maybe I'll figure out how to start a fire, and next Christmas, I can give them the same gift they gave me last year."

"Jack!" shouted Alex.

Johnny slowly raised his head. He glared at Jack.

Johnny spoke firmly. "I've stuck up for you so many times, Jack. I've told others that they just didn't understand you . . . but it was *me*. *I* was the one who didn't understand . . . You really are a *bad* crow."

Jack's eyes widened as he stared at Johnny. This was it. They really were enemies now. Their childhood friendship was gone. Jack shook his feathers and then flew away, back to the fields.

Alex went over to Johnny and put his paw on Johnny's shoulder. After a moment, Alex asked, "What are we going to do? You heard Jack. He promised he'll be back. He's going to try and hurt the house kids."

Johnny turned and looked at the house. "And we'll be here to stop him."

Turn the page to read the
first chapter of book two!

CHAPTER 1

Like Fathers, Like Sons

"Ma? Ma Cow?" Johnny called out. Johnny and his best friend, Alex, were standing in front of Ma's stall door.

"Are you up yet, Ma?" asked Alex.

"Well, bless my soul. Do I hear two proud new daddies callin' for me?" Ma answered as she lowered her head over the door.

Alex beamed as he stood tall with his squirrel chest stuck out. "Yes, ma'am."

"Oh, I've been hopin' you two would come see me! I can't wait to hear all about your new young'uns. A first litter for Alex and a second litter for Johnny! And all born on the same day, I hear!" Ma exclaimed.

"Yes, ma'am, you heard correctly," answered Johnny the rabbit. He smiled over at Alex and said, "You go first."

"We had two kits—a boy and a girl," Alex told Ma.

"One of each! How wonderful! And how's your wife doing? I know she was feelin' anxious about havin' her first litter," said Ma.

"She's doing great! She's such an amazing mom already. I mean, it's like she just knows what they need without anyone telling her!"

"It's those momma instincts! What did you name the sweet babies?" asked Ma.

"Preston and Abigail," Alex answered.

"Now those are two fine names! Yes, they are."

Ma turned her attention to Johnny. Ma's energy changed as she calmly said, "Johnny, I hope I won't upset you, but I wanna ask about what I heard. Word around the farm is that one in your litter struggled. How is that young'un doing?"

Johnny nodded understandingly. "He's okay

now, but it was very touch and go there for a while. I've never been so scared before in my life." Johnny looked down for a few seconds. Ma and Alex waited patiently for Johnny to continue.

Johnny let out a big breath and then looked back up at Ma. "Harriet gave birth to eight kits this time—six girls and two boys." Johnny looked at Ma and then at Alex as he said, "You both know I adore all of my girls, but I was thrilled to see two boys! Six girls in a row and then came the boys— Elliot and then . . . and then Logan . . . our little Logan." Tears came to Johnny's eyes. "Logan wasn't breathing when he was born. He's the runt of the litter." Johnny closed his eyes. "He's so small."

Alex put his paw on Johnny's shoulder.

Johnny sniffed, opened his eyes, and cleared his throat. "I thought Logan was gone, but Cassie . . ." Johnny chuckled as he shook his head back and forth. "Cassie was incredible. She takes her role as our oldest daughter very seriously. She came to help Harriet with the births. Cassie started rubbing on Logan's little chest with her paws. It felt like she did that for an hour, but I'm sure it was only for a minute or so. And then it happened! We heard Logan cough and take a small breath." Johnny looked up at Ma. "Best sounds I've heard in my life."

149

Tears welled in Ma Cow's kind eyes. "Oh, Johnny, how is that darlin' boy doin' now?"

"He's okay. He's tiny and much weaker than the rest, but . . . I just know he's going to be fine," Johnny answered.

"That's right," added Alex. "I know Logan, Elliot, and my Preston are going to be up to fun shenanigans in no time at all!"

"Oh, I know that's the truth! Like fathers, like sons." Ma Cow laughed. "Now when do you two think I'll get to meet all these sweet young'uns? I know squirrels take a bit longer to be out and about than rabbits do."

"Mine should open their eyes in about three more weeks," Alex answered. "I bet they'll be able to visit you a little after spring comes."

"Mine will be ready sooner, but I think Harriet and I will keep ours in the nest a bit longer than usual. That way Logan won't be in the cold, and he'll have time to get stronger before he ventures out," said Johnny.

"I completely understand, sugar," said Ma. "I always look forward to spring comin', but now I'll be lookin' forward to it even more! Thank you both for comin' to see me and for fillin' me in on your sweet babies. Now you two better get on back to your nests. Your wives have their paws full with all those young'uns and need you two at home!" Ma said with a twinkle in her eyes.

"Yes, ma'am!" Johnny and Alex called as they scurried out of the barn.

JACK ᴛʜᴇ Bᴀᴅ Cʀᴏw Sᴛʀɪᴋᴇs Aɢᴀɪɴ

Scan the code to order book two!

JACK ᴛʜᴇ Bᴀᴅ Cʀᴏw Rᴇᴛᴜʀɴs

Scan the code to order book three!

JACK
THE
BAD CROW

If you enjoyed reading this book,
please leave an online review!

Scan the code to leave
a review on Amazon.

Acknowledgements

Thank you to my amazing junior beta readers!

Madelyn Flora

Derek Flora

Gus Chesnut

Abigail May

Preston May

Charley Kate Ealy

Evelyn Ealy

Georgia Haynie

Ellie Teat

Thank you to my equally amazing beta readers!

Alex Flora

Alana Allen

Amanda Allen

Julie May

Taylor Haynie

Lindsey Teat

Alex, Madelyn, and Derek, thank you for inspiring, encouraging, supporting, and loving me. Your imaginations are the best! I love you three!

My grandma, Iva Jo, kept my sister and me many, many nights when we were growing up. She loved us, sacrificed for us, and took amazing care of us.

My dad, John Allen, first introduced my sister and me to Jack (a character made up by his dad) when we were very little. We enjoyed our dad's Christmas stories so much! Dad loved Christmas and always tried to make it the best time of the year.

Captain Maurice Tingle, thank you for reading through the fire scenes and checking the content. I'm blessed to have dedicated firefighters in my family.

I searched for months for the right illustrator, and thankfully, God led me to Kim Sponaugle. Kim, thank you for the beautiful illustrations!

Julie May, you have always been and will always be my go-to graphic designer. You're the best! Thank you for constantly helping me and replying to my numerous texts.

Subscribe to Holly Jo Flora's
monthly newsletter!

hollyjoflora.com

Scan the code to order
Holly Jo's activity book!

Made in the USA
Monee, IL
16 October 2024